What Remains

NICOLE R. TAYLOR

"This is the way the world ends
Not with a bang but a whimper."

T.S Eliot

"Alone. Yes, that's the key word, the most awful word in the English tongue. Murder doesn't hold a candle to it and hell is only a poor synonym."

Stephen King

What Remains

I'd never known true darkness until the lights went out.
And like other people in the first world, I had never known
what it was to be hungry.
Everyone I ever knew was dead. If they weren't, then they
wished they were. I know I did.
I had no idea what kept me going. That somewhere out
there in the waste of human existence, someone was alive.
Someone full of light and hope?
Some people would call this the end of the world. I would
call it hell on earth.
Society had crumbled and chaos ruled. Nature had
reclaimed the earth and human habitation crumbled under
mother nature.
A lot of people died. More people were murdered. Others
just disappeared. If you knew what was good for you, you
left the city behind and hid. People equaled death.
There were no safe zones. The police and army were non-
existent.
No one was coming to save me or anyone else.
We were all on our own.
I was alone.

One

When I saw the column of smoke on the horizon I knew it was time to move again.

This had been my life for the past god knows how long. The less people I saw the better. If I saw no one, that was the way I liked it.

The few that I had met out in the wasteland were no better than thieves and murderers. They were hungry and when people were hungry, they became desperate. In the early days people clogged the roads to get out of the city, but many didn't make it far. They either got sick, starved or were stuck in the Quarantine. There was an eerie lack of abandoned cars and remains on the roads. The government did their job well, I'll give them that. Containment meant everyone, sick or no. The dead were burnt and even if they died from other things, they were treated the same. Doors on the homes of the infected were painted with red crosses. Things had descended into chaos abnormally fast.

I hadn't seen anyone in months. Occasionally, I would come across old tracks or campsites that bore traces of human habitation, but they were old. Anyone who had lingered in those places were long gone. Others had escaped or had been missed out in the bush and those were the ones I was wary of. The fact that people had survived this long - that was all the more reason to avoid them. I had gotten this far by being stealthy. They had gotten this far by murdering and stealing.

Pulling on a battered pair of aviator sunglasses, I tied back my long dark hair, twisting it off my neck and climbed up onto the rickety roof of the house. The ramshackle little cottage in the middle of nowhere. It was falling down, had holes in the roof and no floor, but it was sheltered and there was water nearby. Surveying the landscape, I was satisfied that nothing moved except for the column of smoke. The wind was flat today, the smudge in the distance climbing upwards into the blue. From the looks of it, it was coming from just below the far side of the ridge. Whoever it was wasn't far away and chances were they'd come and investigate the house.

Sitting in the shade cast across the roof by the large gum tree in the yard, I consulted my worn out map weighing up my options. South was out.

In the north there had been many farms, canola, wheat, potato. What was left of them was anyone's guess. It was a lot of flat, open paddocks and little cover. If I went east I would hit a town, a small one, but a town none the less. It would take too much time to go around and the land offered nothing of value. I'd been there before.

West looked best - it was towards the region that was once called the Grampians. The end of a mountain range, a place of rock formations, forest and plenty of places to hide and was once a protected National Park. There was only a small town at the gateway, mostly camp grounds and a few motels and if I didn't linger, I could chance it. The smaller the town, the less chance they would be hiding out there.

West it was.

I busied myself collecting my few possessions and checked it all twice before clipping the kaki bag closed. Taking a branch, I swept the ground clean, careful not to leave any traces to show that I had been there. No charcoal from the fire, no animal bones, the leaves that I had lined the earthen floor with or footprints.

Standing by the door, I picked up my samurai sword. It had a black and yellow hilt and sheath, the guard decorated with a Japanese water dragon. I was like a walking graphic novel, except there weren't zombies in this apocalypse. Only human monsters and the things they'd become. The sword was comfortable across my back, it reminded me of my brother Jase, wherever or whatever he might be now. It was the one thing I had left of the people I'd lost and it'd saved my life countless times over.

Shouldering my pack, I obscured my tracks as I left the house, not ditching the branch until I'd crossed the yard and was over the fence into the field. Whoever those people were, it wouldn't bode well for them to catch onto the direction I went. It would be a few days until I would be satisfied I was alone again.

From what I could tell, it was the tail end of summer, the days seemed to be growing shorter and it wasn't nearly as hot during the day anymore. The sky was still blue and endless and the ground dry and dusty. I hoped it would rain a little more this winter and I could find a place that I could stay a while.

Looking back the way I'd come, I could see the column of smoke dissipating in the early morning air and was suddenly glad that I'd left when I did. The grey smudge was breaking up, which meant the fire was out and its people on the move. I would be a few kilometers away by the time they happened across the cottage.

Sometime in the afternoon, I knew I'd pass by a town and there was no way I could avoid it. Once I saw it in the distance to the right, I knew I would have to veer north once it was at my back.

The shining buildings in the distance glittered like an oasis, but I knew better. It was only a mirage. A smoke screen for the horror that waited for the desperate idiots who dared to go there. They were the only things that lived there, clinging to shadows, the things that lingered in the wake of the survivors. Yeah, it was stupid to go there. I wanted to be as far away from this place as I could before the sun set.

By the time the town had receded into the distance, the sun was dipping low. I wanted to find a place to stop before twilight set in. I'd reached the state forest some time ago, plenty of trees surrounded me now, and it would be easy to find a place that was hidden amongst all the ground cover. I made a bed underneath a fallen gum tree that had slid down an embankment and had created a little hole underneath itself. I would be partially covered above and behind, there was even a decent view down the slope into the gully. I would see anything approaching from the front and hear anything from behind and to the side. I sat for a moment and listened to the forest. The only sound that reached my ears was the rustling of the trees overhead and the odd bird call.

I was alone.

It would be warm enough tonight without a fire. A blanket and a good ground cover of leaves and bark would do the trick. I eased myself into my makeshift bed and massaged my shins. I'd built up a lot of leg muscle with all the walking I did, but I still ached after a days tramp across the hard ground. Need and an empty stomach drove me more than actual strength did.

It would be a long night alone with my thoughts. I pulled a battered copy of *Pride and Prejudice* out of my bag and vowed to read until the light was gone. Was it pride that had rendered the world dead, or was it prejudice? Who the hell knew, right? They both got together in the end and how humanity had crumbled.

I was aiming for the tiny town of Halls Gap. It sat at the foot of the Grampians National Park and was the place I was going to hole up in until I could figure out my next move. Without the threat of people, I could think about winter. Maybe I could find a cave somewhere in the rocks? That sounded like bliss, but without a food source it was more like hell.

The approach to town was like walking through a blackened graveyard. It had been something like eight years or so since bushfires had burnt through this forest and it looked like one had been through since. You couldn't be Australian and not know about Black Saturday or even Ash Wednesday. The worst fires in human knowledge in these parts. People had been burnt alive in their cars trying to flee the fire front. I walked the road where their charred bodies had been found and even though the sky was clear, I couldn't help but look over my shoulder and check the horizon. The trees were still charred black, new growth still sprouting all over their trunks like a furry coat of eucalyptus.

I kept off the main road, sticking to the cover of the trees. It never ceased to amaze me how nature had claimed back the land from humanity. Grass and all kinds of plants grew in-between the cracked asphalt, consuming and taking back what had been built over. Without anyone left to maintain them, the roads had crumbled and broken apart in the heat of summer. In the end, nature was the true ruler of the planet.

Buildings and camp grounds loomed out of the forest, silent and empty. At least I hoped they were empty. There was always a chance they would be hanging out in the shadows, waiting, watching. Always hungry. The things that were born out of death.

Signs of the Quarantine that had marked the last days were littered everywhere. Remains of barriers that had blocked the roads still stretched the breadth of the asphalt. Red x's were painted on almost every door I passed, marking them as infected. Cars had been abandoned or burnt out. Windows were smashed and debris was all over the place.

Everywhere I'd been in the last three years was the same. The evidence of the chaos that had taken the last of us had been one of desperation. By that time, I'd already disappeared. The Quarantine was about to be slammed down around the town I lived in and I'd just made it out. Five more minutes and I would have been dead in a pit somewhere. Maybe I should have been more shocked by it, but now it was just one thing in a long line of horrible stuff I'd had to endure.

Moving between buildings was my safest bet. If someone was around, it would be less likely that I'd be spotted. Leaves crunched underfoot, but there wasn't much I could do about that.

Edging my way between the rear of a Motel and the General Store, I stood on something sharp. There was a loud *twang* and a whoosh of air and before I could jump backwards, I felt something slice through my left thigh and I stumbled in surprise. It was an old trap. Crudely put together and forgotten. The shard of glass and metal tore right through my trousers and through the flesh of my upper thigh. For a sickening moment, nothing happened and I hoped it wasn't real. I bit my lip to stop from crying out. My thigh burned. I slapped a hand over the wound and hissed through my teeth. Bloody hell. There was a lot of blood all of a sudden and I felt woozy.

Pulling a plastic bottle from the side of my pack, I unscrewed the lid and dropped my trousers. The water was tepid, but clean and stung like hell as I tipped it over the wound, washing away the sweat and blood. I stilled my nerves for a moment when I saw how deep it was. Panicking would do no good. I was in this now.

Dropping my pack, I took out an old shirt and began tearing it up into strips. It was so worn it didn't take much and when I had enough, I made a makeshift tourniquet above the gash and wrapped the rest firmly as I could. My hands shook as I shouldered my bag again.

I had to find flowing water and something to stop the bleeding. I scanned the sky for signs of any birds. They flew in formation towards water, maybe if there was a flock of parrots around they might lead me in the right direction. But the sky was empty, save for a few stray clouds.

I remembered coming here for school camp in Year Seven. I was twelve at the time, but I wouldn't forget it in a hurry. It was the worst school camp in the history of school camps. We had to walk in the bush for miles, plant trees and do all sorts of team building 'games'. Behind the camp ground there was a trail up into the rocks and there was a waterfall and creek up there a ways.

I dragged myself through the grounds and saw the sign in amongst the tall grass. It read 700mtrs. Crap. I had no choice, so I kept going along the trail, each step tearing the wound further.

The land was silent around for miles and I couldn't help making a racket as I dragged myself through the bush, every agonizing step echoing off the sheer rock. When the sound of running water reached my ears through the gully, I sighed in relief. I was almost there. As I went to move off again, rock splintered a meter in front of my face and the sound of metal ricocheting across the clay quartz split the stillness.

My eyes widened and I stumbled, jarring my leg. Was that a *bullet*? Heart thumping, I made a run for it to the cover of the surrounding trees, falling behind a rock, my leg throbbing. The only place that could have come from was above.

I wasn't alone.

What now? *Eliminate the threat.*

It didn't take long to ease my way up the side of the gully. I was used to this kind of thing and even with the gash on my thigh, I still managed to do it with some skill. At the top of the rise I saw the shape of a man kneeling between the trees, looking down at the path I'd come up.

I edged closer from behind, carefully placing my feet on rock, avoiding the noisy leaf litter. He hadn't noticed me, still scanning the gully below. I really was too sneaky for my own good, even with a bashed up leg.

He had a sniper rifle. A high tech nasty piece of business. I didn't want to know where the hell he'd gotten that. It seemed to be missing the stand that I knew came with them, he had it resting on one knee, ready to move if he needed to. Oh, he would need to move alright.

He was peering through the scope. Looking for me, I assumed. One more step and my hand was on my sword, the rasp of metal loud in the silence of the bush. He spun around the same time as I drew it all the way, the point of the flat blade pressing into his throat, the nozzle of the rifle pressing into my breast bone. It wouldn't take much pressure to sever a few arteries, but then again, it wouldn't take much pressure to squeeze a trigger.

I stood there and stared at the man, not daring to take my eyes from him for even a second. I balanced my weight onto my right leg and scowled at him. I didn't care who he was, all I wanted to know was what his intentions were.

From the look of him, it seemed like he'd been out in the waste a while. His kaki shirt was dark with sweat, face and hands streaked with dirt. I couldn't see his face properly from the way he held the rifle, but what gave me reason to pause were his eyes. They were clear, like green sand blown glass. When the world went to shit, I was twenty-three. In that life I might have thought the man handsome, but now I only saw him as a threat.

"Don't be stupid," he said, the rifle still aimed square at my chest, his voice loud in the enclosed space of the gully. He spoke quietly, but it still echoed back off the rock. "I don't want to hurt you."

Best thing to do was remain silent. Wherever he had come from, there were others. He was lean, but had muscle mass, which meant he had food. His eyes were bright which also meant he had had a good nights sleep. He couldn't be so well off without there being others.

I refused to move or lower my sword. The moment I did, he would shoot me and take me for all I had. Or maybe he would stay true to his word. Safer to assume, no.

"Do you speak?" he scowled, his eyes flickering to my leg.

I opened my mouth, but snapped it shut again. I hadn't spoken for so long, it was like I had forgotten how.

He went to take a step to the side, but I hissed through my teeth and pressed the sword a little harder into his skin.

"Listen," he said, taking a hand off the rifle. "You're bleeding out. I understand you don't trust me after I took a shot at you, but let me help. I can stop the bleeding."

Like hell you can, I thought to myself.

To my surprise, he slowly crouched down, one hand held up and open, the other lowering the rifle. Was he stupid or just plain mad? My sword followed him all the way down, never leaving his throat. The other hand came up and he was at my mercy. Suddenly, I didn't know what to do. I had all the power. I could stick him and run, or I could trust him. But, trust was an obsolete notion.

"I don't mean any harm," he said, looking up at me. "You need help and I can give it to you."

I hesitated. Don't trust anybody. Where had that little gem of a manifesto gone? Right out the window, that's where.

"Please."

I took a step back, feeling light headed. The blade dropped from the man's throat, but I still didn't lower it. I could feel blood running down my leg, soaking my trousers, running into my boot. This was eating up precious time. I needed to get the weight off my leg and get it elevated, like yesterday.

I felt my vision slipping. Shit. I could not pass out. Please don't pass out. The sword began to shake in my grasp and my skin was becoming clammy. It felt just like that time in year 7 PE when I got hit in the head with a cricket ball. It bloody hurt and I had a huge lump on my head that later bruised something fierce. My vision blurred around the edges and there was an odd hissing sound in my ears like that white noise between radio stations. The moment before you actually pass out, you feel your limbs going limp like a rag doll and your whole body crumbles beneath you. You're always out before you hit the ground. That's how I felt right now and I couldn't stop it.

I was powerless as everything turned to darkness.

Two

I remember when I was seventeen I had to go and get my wisdom teeth out. The dentist said they were rotting from the inside out and that they had to go. He showed me the little x-ray and pointed out their rotten little cores. My Mum took me to the day procedure clinic and they knocked me out with anesthetic. It was the best sleep I ever had, but I'll never forget the sensation of coming to. The darkness that clogged my vision as I struggled to open my eyes, all my limbs heavy and my mind muddled. Well, that's exactly how I felt right now, but instead of the bright white recovery room and the promise of pain meds, there was darkness. A darkness that was only broken up by the orange glow of a small campfire.

The air smelt of wood smoke and eucalyptus and something else. Food.

I scrunched my eyes up in an effort for some kind of clarity. I felt like shit. A hand touched my forehead and instinctively I jerked away, my hand trying to find the hilt of my sword, but it wasn't there. So, I used the only thing that was mine to use. I kicked out with my right leg and my foot came into contact with something soft. I heard a grunt of pain from someone who was definitely male.

"Fuckin' Jesus!" the man cursed as he fell back into the dirt. The man with the gun. I got him right where it hurt.

I looked around wildly for my sword, but caught the glint of firelight on the sheath on the opposite side of the clearing, directly behind the man. As if he'd leave it in reaching distance.

God damn, my leg throbbed.

The man recovered quickly and was holding his hands out in front of him as if he was trying to calm a wild animal. Perhaps I was. God knows I'd done some screwed up stuff in the name of survival. I probably looked like I had been dragged through a hedge backwards.

He shifted his weight to his right and I jerked instinctively at the movement.

"Look, you're wounded and starving. I don't mean to hurt you." His eyes were almost sad, the way he looked at me. "Let me help you."

Of its own accord a tear slipped down my cheek and I brushed it away with a scowl. Showing weakness to a man in the middle of the waste. Anything's fair game. Your body, your stuff, your life.

He sighed, knowing that I wasn't going to reply. "Can you talk at all?"

I didn't dare move. He had plenty of opportunity to slit my throat, but my thigh was bandaged, crudely, but bandaged all the same. He'd cut the leg of my trousers off to get at it. I didn't know if I should be relieved that he didn't take them off entirely. The tattoo that snaked up my leg conjured up an image from before. It was a long time since I had really looked at it. A Japanese style dragon and crane traveled up the outside of my left leg, from the top of my ankle, over my shin and knee to the middle of my thigh, swirling through an autumn scene. Full of black and grey wind and orange and red maple leaves. The tip of the dragon's tail was probably ruined now by the gash.

My eyes flickered back to the man when he shuffled. Could he help me? He'd already done enough by tending my leg. That was a start. If I didn't find food in the next few days, then I would be as good as dead. So, I made a hasty decision.

"Yes." It was hardly audible, but it came out. It was probably the first word I had spoken in months or even years.

The man's head snapped up and he stared at me with those strange eyes of his.

"Are you hungry?" he asked after his shock had worn off. He gestured to a can of something that had been warming by the fire.

I must of had a weird look on my face because a small smile crept onto the corner of his mouth and he took a stick and pushed the can towards me, careful not to make any sudden movements. I reached out and snatched it, holding the hot metal in the blanket that had been laid over me. I looked at the brown stew and sniffed.

"Possum," he said. "Ringtail."

I didn't care what kind of possum it was. I was so hungry I ate greedily, not caring what I looked like. I could still feel the man's eyes on me, glittering in the orange glow of the fire. But, one eye was on the darkness, wasn't it?

As I wiped my face with the back of my hand, he said, "Do you have a name?"

I looked him up and down, taking in his own dirty appearance.

A smiled played at his lips. "I'm Shaw."

Shaw was a surname. Was he ex-military? It would explain the rifle, and the semi-decent aim. He'd known how to bind my leg and stop the bleeding. They had taught that kind of survival stuff in the army, didn't they?

He was waiting expectantly, crouched on the opposite side of the fire. I could tell him anything. Give any name I wanted. I could be a new person. When I was small, I used to hate the name my parents had given me. Prudence. When they used it in full, I knew I was in trouble. But, it was who I was. I couldn't imagine being anyone else.

"Prue."

Shaw smiled at me then for the first time and I almost melted. Fucking hell. Where had he been before the world went to shit? I shrunk back from him then, suddenly aware that he had me weaponless in the middle of nowhere.

He was frowning. "I was going to tell you to get some rest while you can, but you're not going to do that now are you?"

I let my eyes flicker to my sword. How I loved that sword. Shaw knew exactly what I was thinking. "I'm not giving it back to you just yet," he said almost apologetically. "I don't want you to gut me with it. Now that we're on first name basis, that'll cut even more."

Was he joking with me? He cocked his head to the side,

waiting. He was joking with me.

When I didn't speak again, he continued, "Listen, do what you want. I'm keeping watch the rest of the night. At dawn I'm going. I would feel better about it if you came with me. That's a nasty gash on your leg. If someone doesn't see to it, it'll probably get infected." His brow creased into a frown and he ran a hand over the stubble on his chin. He looked conflicted, like he wanted to say something he wasn't sure he should. "Come with me," he said, the note of desperation in his voice unsettling. "There's too few of us left to be afraid of one another. We're good people, Prue. We can help you. Please let me help you."

I almost bawled right there and then. There were more people. Murderers, rapists, thieves... that's what the world had become. After years on my own with nothing but myself, there were others. Good people? The hope and light I had thought extinct? I wanted to believe so much.

I opened my mouth to say something, but I couldn't think of any words. Shaw was right. I wouldn't get very far before I died of hunger or infection. I had no choice, but somehow he knew that if I felt the least bit threatened, I would disappear in the night and never return.

I sunk back down into the blanket and sighed.

"I know my word doesn't count for much, but please at least consider it." He turned to the side, his back to the fire, eyes on the darkness.

He didn't speak to me again and despite my best efforts, I slipped into a restless sleep.

I saw my Mum sitting in her kitchen. Our kitchen. The one I had grown up with, familiar and... well, it was just *home*. They had remodeled while I was living away. I should say, Dad had remodeled. She was just as I remembered, her short blonde hair and wicked smile, always asking if I wanted anything. You look thin, let me make you a sandwich. You're pale, here's some chocolate. Do you want a drink? Do you have enough money? One thing about my Mum, she went on and on, but at least she had my best interests at heart.

She was sitting at the table, flicking through the paper, the dog sitting at her feet, hoping for a crumb to drop to the floor. The solid little black and white Jack Russell that had belonged to my Nan before she passed away. He'd become part of our family and lived with my parents now.

"What do you want to do boxing for, Prue?" Mum always tried to dissuade me from doing anything that would see me hurt. She was probably the nicest person you'd ever meet, but she'd also tell you exactly what she thought. *Exactly*. But she wasn't into physical confrontation or anything that would mark my face.

"I want to do something other than go to work." I worked nights at the local supermarket stacking shelves and spent my days reading and playing Xbox. I was not your typical twenty three year old woman. I hated people and night shift afforded me the avoidance I wanted. It was a boring job, not anywhere near as stimulating as my last one was. I copy edited for a travel magazine and while that sounds just as boring, at least I got to read about exotic places all day. And the office was in London. A long fucking way from my parents kitchen in Ballarat, Australia.

"Go to the pool or something. Or the gym. I bet there's a lot of nice guys there." Mum was always trying to get me to go out and meet people. People meaning men. And a man was not what I wanted at all. A man was the reason I left my life overseas to come back to this.

"Mum, I love you, but seriously." Yeah, *seriously*.

"Prudence Ashford, beating up on men will not get you a boyfriend." And there you have it.

"Mum!" I threw my hands up in the air, exasperated.

"You've been back, what, year and a half now and you haven't once been on a date. Unless..." her eyes sparkled across the kitchen table.

"Mum, seriously. Let up, okay?" I was more than happy in my single life, with my single plate and single knife and fork and one bedroom unit. I was just angry at a lot of things. Boxing just seemed a way to beat the shit out of someone without getting arrested for it.

"How about Pilates?" She was looking through the ads in the local free paper. "Or yoga? There's a place just down the road from here. There's always cars out the front. That would be relaxing, right?"

"I don't think so," I curled my lip in disgust.

"Jason did a cycling thing at the gym, didn't he?" Jase was my older brother by three years. When I was little, I worshipped the ground he walked on and instead of me being in the playpen, he'd get in there with his toys so he could get a little peace. We'd play with transformers and cars, Legos and Nintendo. Cricket in the back yard in summer and swimming at the local pool. We'd ride our bikes up and down the street for hours, only coming inside when Mum or Dad came looking for us. I wanted to be just like him, until he became a teenager and we became interested in different things. He liked techno and house music and I liked books and writing.

"RPM," I said. "It's just cycling on the spot to loud, obnoxious music. No thanks."

"You could ask Megumi, maybe she knows something nice." Megumi was Jase's wife. She was Japanese by heritage, though she'd been born in Australia. As a result, Jase collected samurai swords and Japanese art. They were big into anime. I remembered they had met some years ago at one of those conventions.

"Meg would probably take me out and teach me how to use a sword. You don't want me to take boxing lessons, but you'd let me be a ninja?" I joked, which earned me a slap on the wrist.

"Don't be smart," Mum scolded, but I could see she was trying not to laugh.

She handed me the paper, the headline on the front page reading '*Unknown Virus Claims Ten More*'.

I jolted awake, suddenly aware of where I was. I had fallen asleep. But, I was still alive and Shaw was kicking dirt over the remains of the fire, obscuring the fact that it had been there in the first place. He looked sidelong at me, the eerie dawn light shining oddly on his dirty face. I had been dreaming and if I had cried out in my sleep, he didn't say anything.

The memory of my Mum tugged at me a little. I'd stopped crying a long time ago, but the memories never faded. That life was gone and it wasn't coming back. Everyone was dead. Mum, Dad, Jase, Meg. Even the dog was dead. No use sooking about it. Sooking wouldn't help anybody.

"Your pack is right there," Shaw pointed beside me. He must have moved it there sometime in the night.

Shaw hesitated a moment before he shouldered his small pack and slung the rifle across a shoulder. I still had his blanket and he didn't ask for it back. I pulled myself to my feet, my leg stiff and awkward. I didn't let him know that it stung like a bitch and I kept my face passive.

When I looked up at him, I was surprised to see him holding out my sword, hilt first. I could so easily draw it and cut his arm clean off. He had some balls to put himself in that position. Maybe he did mean it when he said he wanted to help.

I reached out gingerly and grasped the sword by the sheath. A gesture to let him know I wasn't going to stick him with it just yet. Not taking my eyes from his, I slung it across my back, the familiar press of leather across my chest reassuring. He backed away a few steps and waited for me to shoulder my own bag, folding the blanket under one of the flaps.

"It's a few hours walk," he said. "If you're coming it'll be a good day with that leg. *Are* you coming?"

Shaw knew I had no other choice. I merely nodded.

I limped behind him, a good ten meters between us, the reassuring weight of the sword pressing into my back. I grimaced at the pain that shot through my leg with every step and carefully masked my expression whenever he turned back to see if I was still there.

"I can help you, you know," he said.

I sneered at him and he shrugged, turning his eyes forward across the horizon.

We were going north, the morning sun at our right, the sky becoming more blue as the morning progressed with only a few wisps of cloud. Every now and then we came across a fallen fence line that had once separated paddocks or an old country back road. The washed out grass came up to my knees, the ground was hard underfoot which meant there hadn't been rain in a while. The farms here used to house either cattle or sheep before. Ruined farmsteads littered the landscape in the distance, but other than that, there was nothing. The path Shaw took offered little cover, but there wasn't any anyway. At least we would have advance warning if anyone approached.

It was almost midday when I realized my leg was bleeding again and had been for some time. The tickle of a droplet of blood that had begun to trail down my bare leg had pulled my attention. When we reached the shade of a line of trees that served as a wind break in the open fields, I stopped, leaning against one of the old trunks and hissed through my teeth as I realized the wound had been tearing. It had become numb, adrenaline pumping through my body, dulling the nerves. Now that I was aware of it, it began to hurt something fierce.

I had learnt to shut out any weakness a long time ago. I knew it was stupid and my stubbornness would see me killed one day, but weakness equaled death in the waste. I couldn't let my guard drop for one moment.

Shaw had stopped when he realized I wasn't following. When he saw the soaked bandage and the fresh blood trailing down my leg, he tried to hide the worried expression that crossed his features. Why the hell was I following this strange man anyway?

I leant my forehead against the tree and grimaced. Perhaps I should just lay down and be done with it. Bleed out right here. I'd had a good run of it. Survived longer than most.

"We won't get there until just before dark," he said. "You have to let me help you."

And have your filthy hands all over me? No thanks.

The thought must have translated to my face and Shaw grimaced, looking at my leg. "Suit yourself."

Truth was, I didn't want to die. Not just yet. So, I reached down and pulled the bandage tighter, ignoring the searing pain that shot through my leg. Be damned if I let him see how much it hurt.

I began walking again, my expression even and determined. Shaw set off with a frown, but didn't protest.

We crossed another paddock and climbed over a fallen barbed wire fence before I stumbled and fell, my arm jarring as I tried to cushion myself. Rolling over, I grimaced as all the new cuts I had just given myself stung. But my leg throbbed ten times worse.

"Shit." Shaw was beside me, and before I could do anything about it, I was in his arms. I tried to push against him with the palms of my hands, suddenly panicked, but he hissed at me, "For fucks sake. Let me help you."

I didn't have the strength to protest any further. I was up shit creek and I definitely did not have a paddle.

I grimaced as he began to run, his hand grasping my legs close to his body so he would jolt them as little as possible. I was now completely at his mercy and it scared the hell out of me. He could be taking me anywhere. At least when I was able to walk on my own I had a semblance of an out. If I felt like he was going to double cross me, I could slit his throat and be done with it.

My face was jammed up against his neck, and I couldn't help but feel the press of his muscular arm in my back, his other hand on my knee. My left leg was pressed tight against his stomach, staining his kaki shirt red. I couldn't help thinking that he smelt disgusting. He must be strong to carry me and all of our stuff. But then again, I weighed shit all, didn't I?

Every so often, he slowed to a fast walk before pacing out again. I don't know how long he ran, I must have slipped in and out of consciousness a few times, but the sky was becoming dark as the sun set, the first stars shining through.

My head lolled backwards and I swore I saw a gate and several people milling about. An electric light? Was that *music*? I tried to hold on to some kind of consciousness, but darkness took me regardless.

Three

When my vision started to clear, it wasn't into clarity.

At first I didn't know where I was. I was lying in a bed. A *bed*. With a mattress and a doona and a pillow. For three years I'd been sleeping on the ground with nothing but leaf litter to cushion myself. Why was I in a bed?

Trying to focus on the room around me, I couldn't make it out. I was in a bedroom in a house and panic shot through my chest. I couldn't be inside. Shifting, I grimaced as pain burned in my leg. Where was Shaw? I remembered him carrying me. I mean, it wasn't like I had much of a choice, but shouldn't he know not to stay in town?

The murmur of voices carried through the wall and I turned my head to listen. Hell, it was like someone had stuffed it full of cotton wool. God damn, it throbbed.

"That was quite a stir you made running into town like that," said a female voice.

"I wasn't aiming for theatrics." Shaw.

There was a pause before the woman said, "Who knows

what the poor dear's been through."

"She was half dead when I found her."

"God knows what would have happened if you hadn't of been there."

"She would be fucking dead."

"Shaw! Language!"

"It's the truth, Nan."

"No need to use the f-word."

"Sorry."

Shaw's grandmother? What the hell? This had to be some kind of hallucination. I traced my fingers across the top of my thigh, testing the wound, but found it heavily bandaged and the movement made it sting. Okay, so not a hallucination. Taking in the room, it looked normal. Regular. Like before. White walls and framed pictures of flowers. I had been put into a queen bed, a patchwork quilt drawn over me. My clothes had been changed into a t-shirt I didn't recognize and black tartan shorts. And I actually smelt *clean*, like rose petals. I hoped to hell that 'Nan' had done that part.

There was a shuffling in some other part of the house, the scrape of chairs across lino. Muffled voices I couldn't focus on. I felt like throwing up.

It was bright outside, though the blind was drawn, backlit yellow from the sunshine. My head was too fuzzy to concentrate on the conversation any more. There was no way I was moving any time soon, I could hardly lift my arms. Despite the alarm bells ringing in my head, I fell back into a fitful sleep, my brow burning.

I flung open my bedroom closet and started rifling through my clothes. Coat, jumper, shirt, jeans, socks, underwear, scarf, beanie. I jammed what I could into the kaki bag I tore from the top shelf. In the kitchen I upended drawers looking for anything useful. Knife, fork, water bottle, can opener. In the cupboard I yanked out the tinned food and the packet of rice I had never bothered to cook and jammed that into the bag as well.

There was a banging on the front door and my head snapped up and my heart thumped. I didn't know anyone. Who was it?

"Quarantine Officers, open up," a loud booming male voice shouted.

Shit. I went for the back door, the heavy pack on my back, cans digging into my spine. Easing the deadbolt open, I peered outside. Nothing. Unlocking the wire security door, I stepped through, closing it behind me, easing the handle back into place to stop it from rattling. I was alone out the back, but I wouldn't be for long.

"Anyone home?" the voice came again, but this time it was followed with a loud bang. I heard the door splinter and didn't stick around to wait for them. I ran towards the back fence and up onto the old crates my neighbor had left there years ago. Long before I'd moved in, anyway. I was up over the fence and into the lane behind the unit block in a matter of thirty seconds.

"Back doors open," I heard someone say.

Before they could figure out that I'd vaulted the back fence, I ran, the pack slamming into my back painfully. I didn't stop. If I did, I would be trapped. Well, worse than trapped. Shot.

I rounded the corner into the street that backed onto the park and slowed to a fast walk. This road was once an alternate route for trucks and b-doubles. Now it was empty. Silent. Good for me. Scanning the street, it was also devoid of any movement from anyone on foot. Taking a deep breath, I jogged across the open space and made the tree line. I almost expected a shout to follow me, but there was nothing.

I had to get out of town. I had to go bush. That was the only way I was getting out of this. I wasn't sick. I'd be condemned anyway if I stayed.

Crossing the park, I kept to the tree line incase anyone had followed. The only sound was the chirping of parrots and squawking of a flock of Corella's on the oval to my left. The lack of human life was eerie. Saturday sports were usually in full swing. Cricket, soccer, footy. Now, there was no one. A hundred thousand people had vanished just like that.

Two blocks over on the other side was my brother's house. Four blocks after that was the town limit. Quarantine was being imposed right that moment. Did I have time to see if Jase and Meg were still there?

At the opposite end of the park, I waited behind the bluestone fence that separated the green from the urban landscape. The hum of an engine pulled my attention to the opposite end of the street where a huge, wide kaki army truck was rounding the corner. On the top a soldier was stationed, his or her eyes scanning the street. A patrol? When my eyes locked onto the huge gun on top, my heart spasmed. It felt like a military occupation in a war zone, not a quarantine. Things must be real bad. No news, no radio, no electricity, no nothing. This was martial law.

I ducked down behind the fence as the truck drove past, shaken at the sight of the machine gun on the roof. No prisoners. If I was caught escaping, would they shoot me? To contain the virus, yes. Yes, they would. I wasn't sick but as if they'd ask me first.

All the houses across the street had red x's painted on the doors and garages and my heart sank. They'd been through this part of town already. My escape had been narrow, but had Jase and Meg got away in time?

As I came up to their house, I already knew deep down what I would find. The door was smashed in and the windows and doors had been painted with the same red paint that marked every other house in the street. It was too late.

I pushed open the front door and it creaked loudly in the silence, making me crouch to the floor in fright. Nothing moved inside or out, so I stood again, stepping gingerly into the house that was so familiar to me. There was no signs that anyone had been here. Everything was still in it's place. Nothing had been looted. The kitchen was spotless and food was still in the cupboard. In the spare room, I found Jase's collection of manga and art still as he'd left it. Immaculate.

Then my eyes settled on the display case on the far wall. Inside were half a dozen samurai swords. I knew the long ones were called katana, but there were littler ones as well, that made up a matching pair for some. Sliding open the case, I pulled out one that had a sheath with a strap along the length. I would need something to protect myself with. I had no idea how to use a sword correctly, but I remembered a quote from a popular book turned TV series. Stick 'em with the pointy end.

I set my pack down and slung the sword over my back. Deciding I had enough time, I arranged the contents of my bag just so and donned that over the top. Testing the katana, I was able to pull it free from its position with ease. Jase and Meg were gone, but I was still here. Peering out the windows, I weighed my options. Wait until it was completely dark, or make a break for it now in full daylight. I knew there was only one choice. I tested the katana again, just to make sure, before braving the street again.

Stick 'em with the pointy end. I hoped I didn't have to.

When my eyes finally opened again, I was still in the bed and this time it seemed to be night out. My eyes locked on the one thing I was fretting over. My bag was propped against the wall, but my sword was nowhere to be seen. I didn't want anything to happen to that sword.

An elderly lady was sitting in a chair beside the bed, reading a book. When she noticed my eyes on her, she folded the page and drew herself closer.

"How do you feel, dear?"

I just looked at her, wondering when she would disappear.

"Shaw said you were a woman of few words." Her smile was kind.

She took a face washer and dipped it into a bowl of water on the bedside table. Wringing it out, she folded it lengthwise and dabbed it across my forehead gently. I suddenly felt five years old again. I saw my Mum next to me, wiping the sweat from my face that time I was sick with the measles. I didn't have the strength or inclination to protest at this strange woman. Was this 'Nan'?

"You're very ill, dear," she said gently. "You have a nasty cut on your leg, but we got old Doc Howard to patch you up. Oh!" she exclaimed, suddenly. "Forgive me. My name is Gwendolyn, Gwen for short. But everyone calls me Nan. Young Shaw told me your name was Prue?"

I just looked at her like I was going to cry. She was so nice. Why was she so nice?

"Oh, dear," she crooned, when she realized. "You're safe here. You're among friends."

She put the face washer aside and stood. "If you feel okay dear, I will bring you some soup. Put some meat on those bones."

I let myself nod.

Nan grinned, obviously pleased she had someone to care for and left, closing the door behind her.

Could I let myself trust these people? Shaw, Nan and this mysterious Doc Howard, who I assumed stitched my leg back together. How many other people were here? Where was this place? I closed my eyes and sighed. I couldn't even trust myself. Shit, I couldn't even say two words back to back.

When Nan came back with a glass of water and a bowl of warm soup, I felt my stomach churn. She helped me scoot back in the bed, so I could sit up a fraction. I tried to lift my hand to grasp the spoon, but she swatted it away, content to feed me like a child. I felt degraded, but didn't say anything. Once the soup was gone, she only let me take a few sips of water, telling me I would be sick if I was too greedy.

She clucked her tongue at how thin I was and vowed to see me round again.

"When you can put weight on that leg again, I'll have you out and about," she was saying. She had already become accustomed to continuing on when I didn't reply to any of her questions. I was thankful that she never asked about what had happened to me. I didn't want to share. What could I have said in one word sentences anyway? Shit. Horrible. Death.

"You've been sleeping for three whole days, dear," Nan said. "Shaw has been asking after you every five seconds. I swear that boy will be the death of me." She smiled at me, trying to gauge my reaction from the expression plastered on my face. "He's one of the good ones. I'm glad he was the one who found you."

Despite every bone in my body telling me to run, I found myself liking this woman. She was gentle, understanding and surprisingly *normal*. Seeing her sit there and talk without a worry in the world, it reminded me of my own grandparents. And she was still going on like there was no end to the things she wanted to tell me.

"He said he ran almost six k's carrying you. Six k's! Can you believe it? He's a strong boy, our Shaw." She fussed with the patchwork quilt, pulling it up over my leg. "You'll like the town, dear. I do hope you'll decide to stay when you're well. There's plenty to keep busy with and everyone is nice enough."

A whole town? How was that possible? Why weren't they dead?

"Doc Howard is coming round to check on you in the morning. He's a nice man, dear and he'll be pleased to see you awake. Until then, you should get as much rest as you can. You had a terrible fever, but thank goodness that's finally broken." Nan collected her book and the dishes and stood. "If you need anything, just call out, okay dear?"

When I didn't respond, she just smiled and closed the bedroom door after her.

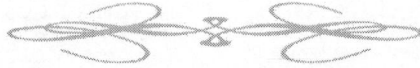

Doc Howard was a middle aged man with salt and pepper hair and a kind disposition. He told me that he'd stitched my leg when I was unconscious as they didn't have anesthetic anymore. Thirty six stitches. He didn't know how I had walked so far without passing out earlier. It seemed Shaw had told them everything, though I wondered if he'd said anything about trying to shoot me.

Doc Howard had been the town GP before, and had delivered a few babies in his time and patched up a whole lot of nasty farm injuries. He did an internship at one of the big city hospitals, but said he preferred the bush. People were nicer here, they cared to learn everyone's names. And they were in a lot less of a hurry.

Since the town had a lot of animals, he also substituted as the town vet when he could. Birthing calves and lambs, that kind of thing. He seemed to like talking as much as Nan did and didn't seem to mind my silence at all. He passed the time by telling me about the town, like he was delivering a sales pitch.

Why did they want me to stay so bad?

"Are you into animals? We've got a nice size herd of Jersey cows and even horses. I know Hannah'd love a bit of help with the chooks."

I just raised my eyebrows.

"No chickens?" he joked.

I shrugged.

"Milking cows is rather relaxing once you get the hang of it."

"Oh, shoosh, Tom," Nan said. "How's Prue's leg?"

"The gash wasn't that deep," he said with a chuckle, "but a vein was severed, which caused the bleeder."

I just looked at him with a frown. That didn't sound so good.

"It'll heal quickly now that you have time to rest."

I nodded.

"A week should do it, but keep off it as much as you can." He pointed to the set of crutches against the wall. "If you need to get up, keep your weight off. We don't want to pop any stitches. Try and keep moving if you can manage it, otherwise your muscles will weaken."

These people seemed to genuinely care. I mean, I wasn't dead and all my stuff was here. They'd even fed me. But, I still wasn't sure what I was meant to do. My head told me to make a break for it, but my heart told me to drop my guard. Which one was I meant to listen to?

When Doc Howard was done, he left with a wide smile that looked like he was trying to over do it with kindness and left Nan in the room with me.

"I really do hope you decide to stay, Prue," she said. "Out there is no place for a young woman. I don't know what you've had to go through, but know that you can trust us. We want to help. All of us."

I thought about Shaw. He'd said the same thing. I thought about Doc Howard. He'd had one hell of a sales pitch. Maybe Nan was right? I really hoped she was because truthfully? I was tired. I was so tired, I could just lay down and die. If Shaw hadn't of found me, I would have done just that.

Was this my second chance at life? I closed my eyes with a sigh and hoped to everything that was good in the world that it was.

Four

It was a week before I felt well enough to stand on my own. Even though the fever had broken, I'd lost a lot of blood and that had knocked me around the most. Nan filled me up with as much food as she could manage, even though they seemed to have strict rations. I hadn't seen anything of the town, but Nan said they had crops and animals. Their own little farming community, she called it. It seemed impossible with all the shit out there in the waste and I didn't dare believe it until I saw it with my own eyes.

On the afternoon of the seventh day, Nan helped me to the front porch and sat me in a patio chair. In what used to be the front yard, was a large vegetable patch and on the other side of the path from the road to the door was a rose garden, which was in full bloom. Form and function, Nan called it.

I hadn't seen Shaw since he brought me here, so when I felt his eyes on me I was suddenly shy. He was standing on the footpath gazing at me across the rose bushes. I shouldn't feel anything around him. On a bad day I could be a match for him. I bet I could kick his ass.

"I can see you hovering there, Shaw," Nan sighed loudly and waved him over.

He stomped up the stairs and leant against the side of the house, crossing his arms. "I see you're finally feeling better," he said when no one was forthcoming.

"Doc Howard says that the stitches will come out the day after tomorrow," Nan proclaimed.

"That's great news." Shaw looked at Nan with a raised eyebrow.

She got it after a second and laughed. "I'll go inside and give you kids some privacy."

When the screen door banged closed behind her, Shaw sat on the chair she'd vacated. It didn't escape my notice that he had done it on purpose. He didn't want to scare me or block off my only escape route.

"So," he said, running a hand through his hair.

I just looked at him, like a stupid fool. Shaw cleaned up well. And when I say well, I mean *really* well. Where his hands and face before were streaked with dirt and stubble coated his face, he was clean shaven and polished. As if that was even a way to describe someone who'd had a bath. His eyes were still oddly green and clear, but they stood out more when he was dirty. Jesus H. Christ, I scolded myself. I was checking him out? Had I completely lost my mind?

"I know you can speak," he grinned lopsidedly, startling me out of my blatant perusal. "I've heard you say two words. One of them being 'yes' which is quite an agreeable word if you ask me."

He seemed not to notice the pun.

"I can see a million questions running about that pretty

head of yours, but you'll just have to ask them if you want to know the answers." Before, in my old life, I would have told him to go fuck himself. In this one, I just frowned and looked away. He was spot on and it was annoying.

"Nan says we should throw a welcoming BBQ for you once you feel up to it. Really, it's just an excuse to have a party. Though, I'm not sure about that," he squinted as he looked up to the sky, the sun beginning to creep onto the porch.

I grimaced. The idea of a party sounded frivolous.

"Everyone is keen to meet you, Prue. But, you've gotta say something to them to be polite." He was trying to get a response out of me. I should give him points for trying. Truth was, I found talking exhausting and the thought of all the people that must live here was overwhelming. That was the nail in the coffin. That many people kind of scared me.

I opened my mouth, but closed it again. I didn't have anything to say. Trying to think of something exhausted me as much as talking would.

Shaw sighed and stood. "I'll get something outta you eventually. But right now, I've gotta go to the wall."

I cocked my head to the side as if I asked him a question.

"Watch," he said, understanding. My interest didn't go unnoticed and he laughed. "If you want to know, just ask."

I rolled my eyes as he walked down the front path. As he passed by on the footpath, he raised a hand in a wave. I felt myself kind of liking him. I didn't know what the other people here were like, but Shaw and Nan, they seemed okay. Even Doc Howard.

Why didn't I want to speak? Maybe there was nothing left

worth saying. Nothing good anyway. As I watched him disappear down the street, Nan came back out, giving away that she'd been eavesdropping in the hallway.

"I swear that boy has developed a crush on you," she said with a smile.

I looked at her as if to say, *he must be mad* and she laughed. I suppose it was nice that he'd come to see if I was okay. That was a decent thing to do, wasn't it?

He was handsome enough, but having a crush at the end of the world was more trouble than it was worth. There were bigger things to worry about than what some guy thought about me. I was something new and the same thing would happen to me that happened to all new things after a while. I'd soon get old.

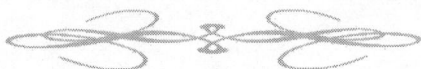

Later than night, I was able to make my own way out to the kitchen on the crutches Doc Howard left for me. It also gave me an opportunity to look at the house a little more closely. The fact that Nan had left me alone to my own devices was evidence of the great deal of trust they'd put into me. Either that, or they knew I had no chance of escape. So, that was one of the reasons I didn't go looking for my sword. I hoped they'd give it back eventually. It was the only thing I had left of my brother.

Most of the house had hardwood floors that had been stained a deep, rich mahogany and the walls were a warm, creamy white. As I made my way down the hall towards the sounds and smells of cooking, I passed photo upon photo.

The people in them seemed to be relatives or friends of Nan's. Some were black and white and had that old feeling about them. That one had a 1960s looking car with a young girl sitting on the bonnet. Another looked like a formal dance portrait, the same girl and a guy smiling back. Echoes from a dead world.

I didn't look at anymore, making my way through the house, the crutches clacking on the floor every time I took a step. Stealth was beyond me today.

The kitchen reminded me of an old country home. A farmer's home. Cream colored cupboards lined the walls over the sink, the floor was covered with slate grey lino and frilly, floral and lace curtains covered the windows. Every now and then a bare patch of wall had been decorated with a framed drawing of some farm related animal. Cows, chickens, that kind of thing.

There was a round dining table in the middle of the room, a bright red and white tablecloth on top and place settings for two already set out. In the middle was a glass with a peach colored rose from the garden out front. It was so homely, it almost made me forget that outside, the world was a piece of shit.

Nan heard me shuffle into the room and smiled at me, a wooden spoon in her hand. "It's really nice having you out at the table, Prue," she said, fussing over the stove. It was one of those old fashioned ones with a place to put in a fire, so cooking inside was no problem. The house seemed to be rather old. Stuck in the 1800s.

I watched her cook and I wondered if I should get up and help, but she seemed to be on top of it. I'd become very familiar with cooking over an open fire.

"It's a quiet life, but there's not much opportunity for

career development," Nan laughed at her own joke. "Unless you want to get into farming, doctoring or even electrics. They always need help at the shop with the solar panels." She was working on the sales pitch again.

I wondered what Shaw said about going to this mysterious wall. Soldiering, wandering, scavenging. Those were things I knew how to do.

"There's always something to do," Nan continued. "There's the school, too. Some of us go and give miniature lessons about useful things we can remember."

School? There must be children here. I wondered how many.

"Were you alone for a long time?" Nan asked carefully.

I nodded.

"Since the beginning?"

I nodded again.

"Oh, my dear," she exclaimed. "No wonder you don't want to talk. You didn't have anyone to talk to."

I shook my head. I had to say something eventually. I was certainly capable of it. After all, I'd said two words to Shaw. When Nan placed my share of dinner in front of me I had a go. "Thanks."

It came out so quiet, I wasn't sure if I'd said it at first. But when Nan almost fell over, I knew it was real and I think I just gave her a heart attack. "You're welcome," she said after a few seconds. She sat at her place opposite me, stirring the vegetable soup she'd made, suddenly quiet. "You know you can talk to me about anything."

I hesitated. I didn't want to lump that on this nice old lady. No one should have had to live like I did, but it was necessary. I didn't want to talk about it. People seemed to think that talking and sharing would heal any hurt inside of you. This wasn't like a tragic accident or a sad domestic violence story. It was life. It was the way the world was now and I didn't want to talk about it because what was there to talk about?

I'd done some nasty things, but only ever in self-defense. Maybe I was coping too well with it and what kind of person did that make me? These people wanted me to stay in their town, but did I really belong in it? Did I deserve to?

What it boiled down to was necessity. Life or death. That was the only choice I had to make and right now, I wasn't sure which.

Two months after Quarantine.

Bush survival one-oh-one.

Step one. Smell it. If it smells like peach or almonds, don't eat it.

Step two. Put berry juice on the inside of your elbow or the corner of your mouth. If it reacts, don't eat it.

Step three. Taste just one. If you're sick after a few hours, don't eat it.

Step four. Birds fly in formation towards water. Especially parrots. When they fly away, it's all over the place. You can extract water from greenery by placing a plastic bag over a branch and sweat it out on a hot day. You can collect dew from plants in the early morning in winter. Never drink water from a creek unless you boil it first.

Step five. Never sleep on the bare earth, it'll sap your warmth. Make a bed of leaves.

Step six. Never, ever burn green wood. It'll cast a plume of dark smoke a mile high and bring anyone who's watching right down on top of you.

And always, I mean always, keep an eye out for trouble.

In the beginning I broke almost all of those rules. If it wasn't for my fear of being discovered, I would have died in my sleep a hundred times over.

Why the hell did I keep going? My Dad told me something the day I left that would stay with me forever. He said, *Have faith. Keep going. Things will get better, you'll see.* If it wasn't for those words, I would have given up a long time ago. The fact that my parents wanted me to live? That had to mean something. Even if I'd lost parts of myself along the way, it had to.

I'd become quite good at moving silently through the bush. My gut had told me to stay off the roads and if I had to stray near, keep to the brush. I couldn't remember the last word I'd spoken. It was probably some curse word. Shit. Fuck. Right up there in the memorable section on Wikiquotes. The last words of Prudence Ashford: *Fuck.*

Through the undergrowth, I spotted one of those wooden signs. You know, the ones you find in National Parks. X amount of k's to whatever-waterfall or camp ground. This way to the hole in the ground that served as a public toilet. One of those. This one said five hundred meters to a camp ground and my hackles suddenly rose and my gut tingled.

Any hint at civilization made that dark place inside me cringe in fear. Nothing good could come of it.

For only two months since the town had shut down, it had been eerily quiet. I'd seen people to begin with. On the roads in their cars, trying to run from the army or whoever wanted to rob them blind. Now, there was a lack of anything. It was like I was the last human left on earth, but somehow I knew that wasn't right.

Despite all my fears, I decided to check out the camp grounds. Maybe I'd find something useful. When my stomach gurgled, I thought I might find something to eat, though that was doubtful.

The sky was grey in-between the treetops and the air was cool. Winter was fast approaching and I knew I had to find somewhere warm and some kind of food to last.

Moving through the low-growing ferns, I approached the camp grounds at a snail's pace. As I neared, I caught sight of color through the shredded trunks of the huge ghost gums that dotted the clearings. Someone was here, or had been. Stuff was littered everywhere. A shredded tent was at one end of the site, clothes and an assortment of pots and pans were strewn in the mud along with some trash and other bits of camp gear. Whoever had been hiding out here had been set upon by someone. Surveying the area, I decided it was clear and moved out into the open.

Picking through the remains of the camp, I quickly realized nothing useful was left. I had to get away from here incase someone was coming back. I turned to go the way I'd come when I heard a rustling sound behind me. My hand was on the hilt of the sword so fast, the ring of metal as it flew from the sheath split the air menacingly. Twisting around towards the sound, the tip came face to face with a small grey wallaby.

"Shit," I hissed as it looked up at me with it's small brown eyes. My heart thumped painfully in my chest as I took a deep breath to calm myself. The thing must be so used to people camping here it had come to see if I would feed it.

That's when I heard the footfall behind me and I instantly knew that it wasn't an animal. Well an animal, but of the human variety. I turned again, the sword shooting around in an arc and I almost stumbled when I saw how close I'd just come to being deader than dead. A man stood two paces behind me, a nasty looking carving knife in his hand. I didn't stop to take in his appearance, because at that moment he went to lunge, but my sword was still in full swing. I didn't want to die. Not like this.

He was desperate and so was I.

As the man stabbed upwards, I arced my sword across, the edge slicing into the skin of his neck. Nobody tells you about this part. Before. After. Not during. How slicing into someone was like slicing butter. It was over so quickly, I was dazed.

The man dropped the knife and fell to his knees with a surprised grunt, blood pouring from the wound in his neck. When he hit the ground his eyes glazed and I knew he was dead.

You could say it was him or me. You could say it was survival. It was all of those things and more. But, I'd still done something that I thought I'd never have to do. I looked down at the sword in my shaking hand and the silver metal was streaked with red. I looked around me, wild eyed, hoping he was alone and when I was greeted with silence, I heaved a sigh of relief. Then I high-tailed it out of there incase anyone came looking.

Running through the bush, I felt tears begin to fall down my flushed cheeks, the sword trailing behind me, still coated with what I'd done. I was a fraud, a phony, a *monster*. I hated what the world had forced me to become. I hated what the world had forced that man to become. It wasn't fair. No one deserved it.

I'd just killed a man and I'd never be the same again.

Dad? I thought as I put one foot in front of the other, running from the carnage. *You said things would get better. You said to have faith. You never said I'd have to kill to get there.*

Five

Nan told me that Doc Howard was coming this morning to take the stitches out of my leg.

And what a relief that was. She confined me to bed until he came, giving me a book to read and a plate of home made bread that she'd toasted on the open fire and some blackberry jam and a glass of milk. I was really quite surprised at how they'd come to have such things. Blackberry bushes were considered a weed and they grew everywhere unchecked, but now it seemed they were useful.

They really had a production going and I found myself wanting to see it for myself. The fear that had built up inside me when Shaw had tried to convince me to come here was all but gone. No one had tried to hurt me or hold me against my will. They'd cared for me and shared their food. They'd trusted me and I'd started to trust them. Somehow I knew I was safe here.

When Doc finally came, he had brought someone along with him and I was suddenly wary. Three people were three too many after being alone for so long. Adding a fourth to the mix was getting a little overwhelming, but I knew if I was going to stay here, I'd have to deal with a lot more than four people.

"This is Hannah Robertson," Doc said, gesturing to the girl in the doorway. "She's my apprentice and she handles the chooks."

I looked over at her, nervous at another new face, but she smiled warmly and said, "Hey. Nice to meet you."

Hannah was tall and slim like me, but had long mousey brown hair that had a kink to it and a kind face. She had a dark floral dress on and work boots and I got the impression she wasn't one of those girly girls. She looked like she'd grown up in the country.

"Hi," I said and I almost thought they'd all missed it but Doc looked at me in surprise. As if he knew, he ignored the fact that that was the first time he'd heard me speak and gestured for me to sit up.

I scooted up the mattress, my back against the headboard of the bed that had unofficially become mine and Nan held my leg up as Doc Howard began to unwind the bandage. As the pressure lifted from the wound, it felt a little tight, but there was no pain. When cool air kissed my skin, it felt like heaven. I'd never broken a bone before or had an injury like this, so having to be off my leg for so long and have it wrapped up was the most annoying thing ever. You never miss something until you can't use it anymore. I relished the feeling of freedom.

"Good, good," Doc said, inspecting the stitches and the puckered line that was once the gaping gash on my leg. I knew instantly that it would scar in a pink jagged line right across the top of my thigh. Hannah was looking over his shoulder as Doc inspected his handiwork, her eyes running the length of my leg inspecting my tattoo.

"It'll scar, dear, but there's nothing we can do about that," he said when he saw me looking.

I nodded. It wasn't like he was a plastic surgeon and to be honest, I didn't really care that much.

"Now," Doc said, taking up a pair of long tipped scissors, "this won't hurt, but it'll probably feel a little weird."

He slid the end of the scissors through each stitch and clipped each one. All thirty-six. When he was done, he took out a pair of tweezers and pulled each from my skin. He was spot on when he said it would feel weird. As each little piece came free, I tingled, but it was over as quickly as it had started.

Doc gave me the run down. "You'll need to go easy on it for a few weeks still. No strenuous activities, no walking long distances."

That meant no training. No checking out what this mysterious wall business was and definitely no finding out what it was that Shaw did out in the waste. Then what could I do?

"There's plenty of things that you could help out with," Nan said kindly. Maybe she got it.

"You're welcome to help me with the chooks," Hannah said. "Or with the boys in the milking shed."

"Oh, yes," Nan exclaimed. "Hard on your back, but it'll keep you off your leg until it's right again."

"If you're up to it, Hannah will take you around the town," Doc said. "It's not a huge place, and the walk will do you good."

I nodded, then remembered my manners. "Okay."

"Great," Hannah beamed.

Once I'd pulled my boots on, she led me outside and I was grateful for the fresh air and the lack of crutches. I'd been here almost a week and a half and I hadn't been outside on my own yet. I think I was a little worried about it, being the new person in town. A curiosity. I wasn't sure what to expect and I hesitated at the edge of the porch.

"C'mon," Hannah gestured for me to follow her down the footpath. "Everyone's keen to meet you, but they won't mob you or anything."

I smiled thinly. I hoped not.

We walked side by side down the quiet street and if you didn't mind the lack of movement or noise, it almost felt normal. Like nothing had happened and the world was right. The distinct lack of cars parked anywhere was a tip-off though, and it just made the place feel off somehow.

"We were lucky in the beginning," Hannah said, breaking the silence. "I grew up here, so I can tell you it was a small place to begin with. We weren't hit that hard with the virus. We have Mayor Thompson to thank for that. Our Quarantine kept it out, not the other way around."

"Lucky," I agreed. I'd been a part of the other type of Quarantine. The bad one. Thankfully, Hannah had the sense not to ask me any questions.

"When news stopped coming and the electricity went out, everyone kinda knew that that was it. We had to stick together and figure out what to do. Some people decided to leave and some decided to stay. Those who stayed helped build the town into what's here now. We never saw anyone who decided to leave again. In the first few months people came and some stayed. Like Shaw and a few of the boys on the farm and the wall. Sarah and Tim Smith came early on too, and they had their little daughter, Renee not long after. Some not so nice people, too."

"What happened to them?" I asked and almost surprised myself with the uninhibited question.

"They caused trouble and some we had to kick out. Some just left on their own. They never came back. Though, I reckon if they saw what we've built now, they wouldn't be so quick to go. We didn't have the wall then."

"What's the wall?"

"I'll show you," she pointed towards the end of the street. "This way."

We passed a few streets with some nice houses, most of them looked lived in. It was a typical small town on the outside. Some newer kinds of homes along with some old weatherboard miner's cottages and some stone buildings that looked official. And there was even a park with a swing and slide, sponsored a long time ago by the local Rotary Club.

As we walked, Hannah kept talking, not bothered by my lack of response. "We have a town council and everything. There's the mayor, Brian Thompson. Grace Howard is on it, too. She's Doc's daughter. She takes care of the shop most days and anything that needs repairing. Jason Ross looks after the farm and makes sure it all runs okay. He was a big time farmer before. Captain Wallis is in charge of the wall and is like our head of security, if you know what I mean."

We rounded a corner and were suddenly facing a dead end.

"This is the wall," Hannah said, rapping her knuckles on the corrugated iron. Above us a platform had been built that ran the entire length, at least the part that we could see from here, and I assumed they must walk it now and then.

"On the other side, they've lined the ground with barbed wire and other nasty things. You can't be too careful these days. There isn't enough of us to protect every inch of the wall all the time."

I scanned the platform and caught sight of a man walking towards us.

"That's Bobby," Hannah said, catching sight of him, too. "They patrol the perimeter every so often, just in case."

When he came closer, he saw us looking up at him and he called out, "Hey, Hannah. How's it going?"

"Hey," she replied, shifting back and forth on her feet. "This is Prue."

"Hey, Prue," he called down to us. "Welcome to our little town. Hope Hannah's treating you okay and not telling tales about us."

I shook my head. "No. Not yet." He seemed nice enough, and handsome. Shaggy brown hair and taught muscles.

Hannah laughed and I swore she blushed a little. "Stop it, Bobby. Of course I haven't."

He just shook his head, a sly grin on his face. "If you say so. I'll catch you girls later." He gave us a small wave and continued down the platform, his eyes fixed over the fence and out into the bush. This was what Shaw must have meant the other day when he said he had to go to the wall.

To my surprise, Hannah threaded her arm through mine

and lead me back to the street like we were already best friends. I didn't mind, but the gesture was still alien.

"We have a school in the old post office building. The park next door has a playground with swings and a slide, so it seemed the logical choice. There's a few kids in town and we teach them to read and write, maths and stuff. Some of the townspeople come and do talks and teach what they can." She pointed to the old brick building and I noticed a carved piece of bluestone at the top that read, Est.1898.

It must have been recess because the side door opened, letting out a few kids of various ages. A blonde haired woman came after them and watched with her hands on her hips as they all pounced on the playground.

"That's Eva Thompson," Hannah said curling her lip.

"You don't like her?" I asked, looking the woman over. I got the impression she was one of those do-gooder sorts. School teacher. Pretty knee-length dress. Immaculate hair even for the end of civilization.

"She's the mayor's daughter."

"Oh." I got it.

"Likes the power trip of being daddy's little girl." She turned to me, her expression serious. "Just be careful around her, Prue. She's got the reputation of being a snake in the grass. Just be careful where you step."

I knew all about her type. I'd come face to face with a few Eva Thompson's in my time. I frowned a little at the thought of coming under her scrutiny, which being new, I no doubt would at some stage. I was the kind of person who always came out second best. Mental note. Stay away from Eva Thompson.

Before the mayor's daughter could turn around and see us, Hannah led me down the main street away from the school and pointed out a few other buildings.

"That's the store," she pointed to the old milk bar that still had all of its signage intact. "It's mostly used as a warehouse. If anyone needs anything you just go there. Clothes, soap, toothpaste, that kind of thing. There and the fish'n'chip shop next door are the only places in town with electricity. Because they run the freezers, all the solar panels that were in town were rigged to the roof. In the beginning, some of the men went out and scavenged panels from around and brought them back. If you want something charged up, you have to beg for it, they don't get a lot of spare juice from them, especially in winter. Some people have iPods and those book readers. They usually have to pull double time or do something that needs fixing before they can use any spare electricity, but."

As the morning wore on into lunch time, I found myself liking Hannah. She didn't seem to care one bit that I answered her in short sentences or not at all. She was like Nan in a way. She liked to fuss and make sure I was taken care of.

Next on the list was the farm, which was on the far side of town to the houses. The milking shed was a long corrugated iron building that looked like it had been constructed haphazardly. Hannah confirmed that they'd built it after the wall went up. If they needed to protect the herd, they could bring them inside. Outside, on what looked to be a footy oval in a past life, they'd put up fencing and a gate at one end in the wall itself.

"There's paddocks outside the wall," Hannah said, following my gaze. "We have guys on the wall who keep an eye on them during the day and at night, they come inside."

"How many are there?"

"They have about a hundred head at the moment. All Jersey's. That's pretty small, but at first we didn't have that many. It's taken this long to build them up. And there's about fifty head of sheep. They come in handy for their wool. The farm's probably the most important thing we have. Most of us work here all year round and during harvesting and planting, everyone is expected to help. Come the middle of summer, we go out in teams to bale hay from the surrounding paddocks, too."

Wow. They really had a thriving community. Luckily for them, a lot of the people who'd ended up here were country folk and had some kind of trade. I wasn't sure how exactly I could contribute, but there was probably some menial task that I could handle.

Hannah pushed open the door to the milking shed and whistled, the sounds and smells of cows filling my nose. Hay, animals and crap.

A young man stuck his head out of a stall at the end and when he saw us inside the door, jogged up to meet us. He wore a flannel shirt rolled up to the elbows, dirty jeans and a pair of work boots that had seen better days. Short cropped rusty red hair and a lopsided smile topped it all off.

"Prue, this is Greg, one of the guys who works with the animals."

"Hey," he said, sticking his hand out. "Nice to meet you."

Since I was trying out this whole, 'be assertive and not crazy wild woman of the waste' thing, I took his hand and shook.

"I'm giving her the grand tour, now that the stitches are out of her leg."

"Oh, shit, yeah," Greg said, looking back at me. "Hope it's okay and not giving you any trouble."

I shrugged. "It's a lot better, thanks."

He smiled warmly and I wondered how much they had been told about me. Probably all the main dot points. Like how I was alone for three years. How I almost died. You know, the important stuff that meant I was delicate.

"I was telling Prue before how you guys might need some help with the milking. Doc says she should keep off her leg for a little while yet, just in case."

"Oh, yeah?" His eyes lit up at the notion of another pair of hands. "We do it all by hand, so shit yes."

I found myself smiling a little at his reaction. "Sounds okay."

"We milk every morning before they go out," Greg explained. "Sixty-odd heifers takes us a few hours, so if you wanna come help, we won't say no. I'm doing the last couple now. Jason and Paul have gone out in the paddock, or I'd introduce you to them. Jason runs the place."

"When he says Jason runs the place, he really means he keep those boys under control," Hannah laughed. "They like to run riot any chance they get."

"Hannah," Greg blushed, giving away that she was right on the money, "stop telling stories."

She waved him off with a chuckle. "C'mon, Prue. We've still got a few things to do."

Greg began backing away towards the stalls at the end of the shed. "Watch out, Prue," he laughed. "That one likes to tell tales."

"Oh, shut your face," she grumbled, closing the door behind us and shutting out Greg's laughter.

We continued the walk around town, the few people we came across waving and saying hello. So far, no hostile looks or pity parties.

"That's Mayor Thompson's place," Hannah pointed to the old looking homestead style house. "He wants to meet you."

My eyes widened a little at the thought of meeting the man who ran the town. When he got an eyeful of me would he kick me out?

"He's a nice guy," Hannah said. "You can understand why he wants to meet you. You're the first person who's come here in over two years. This is monumental."

Brian Thompson turned out to be kind of nice. I think some part of me expected him to be sitting behind a mahogany desk with a suit and tie on, but he sat us down in his kitchen with a cup of tea and homemade biscuits. I think I sat there staring at those for ten minutes before I worked up the courage to try one.

"I can't say how glad we all are that you pulled through, Prue," the Mayor said, watching me poke at the plate of sweets.

"Thank you," I said meekly. He was middle aged and wore a flannel shirt, which seemed to be all the rage with the men in town, with patched up jeans and he had a nice smile. A politician's smile.

"These are dark days we live in," he said. "But, we make the most of what we have and have come out stronger for it.

I'm sure you understand the sentiment."

"Yes," I said. Of course I did.

"It's the fact that we work together and share that we are in such a strong position. Everyone contributes and everyone is cared for. Don't mistake us for some kind of Communist outpost," he laughed. "We run things here democratically. Everyone has a say as to what happens. Everyone."

I nodded again. Like there was any alternative. I looked over at Hannah who smiled warmly at me. Everyone I'd met so far didn't seem to have an issue. They all seemed happy. Maybe I could be, too.

"You're welcome to stay, of course," the Mayor continued. "But, you'll be expected to contribute in some way."

I nodded again. "I've offered to help with the milking."

"Great," he declared.

"Sir?" I asked quietly. "May I have my sword back?"

"Oh," he exclaimed. "That's right. I'm sorry we had to take it from you. Hopefully you can understand why."

"Yes, but," I hesitated a moment. "It was my brother's." I failed to add that it had saved my life more than once.

Mayor Thompson frowned. "Gwen has vouched for you and Doc. Even Shaw. Can we trust you, Prue?"

I didn't know what to say to that. I was so wrapped up in trusting them, I never saw it the other way round.

"We can trust her, sir," Hannah declared. "I reckon you should give it back. If it was her brother's then it's more of a sentimental thing, right?" She looked at me for confirmation and I wondered if she was telling the truth or making up a fib so I could get it back.

Truth was, it was the only thing I had left of my family. I could only nod.

Despite his reluctance, Mayor Thompson slid his chair back and disappeared from the room. A moment later he returned, my sword in his hand.

"Don't make me regret giving this back," he said, like he was the school principle disciplining a naughty student.

"No, sir." I reached out for it, the familiar feel of its weight in my hand reassuring. Having it back was a huge relief. That sword gave me a sense of security and it was more than capable of delivering it if need be.

"Doc says she needs to give her leg another few days, just to make sure," Hannah said, changing the subject.

"Well, you need to follow doctor's orders," he said warmly. "In the mean time, you girls get over to the shop. Pick out whatever you need, Prue. Clothes, boots, anything you want."

I looked at Hannah, unsure. That seemed like a generous offer and I wasn't sure he was serious.

"I'll take you," she said. "I love to shop."

The mayor laughed at her enthusiasm. "Don't go overboard."

"No, sir," she said and pulled on my arm.

"Oh and Prue," the Mayor called out before Hannah could haul me out the door. "If you need anything, or if you need to talk, or someone gives you any trouble, my door is always open."

"Thank you, Mayor Thompson."

Hannah led me the three blocks back over to the shop. Opening the door she pulled me through into shelves lined with boxes and instinctively, my heart began to pound in my chest. Don't go into the dark. Never go into the dark.

"Not exactly Target," Hannah laughed, "but close enough."

"Hello?" a female voice called from the back and I started.

"It's Hannah and Prue."

A young woman emerged from a back room and smiled when she saw us and my irrational fear began to subside. "Hey, I'm Amy Wallis," she said when she saw me. "My dad is Captain Wallis 'head of security'." She air quoted the last bit.

Amy was petite, long brown hair and in terms of looks, plain. But, that didn't mean that much to me. She seemed nice enough.

"Mayor Thompson sent us over to pick out some new things," Hannah said, pointing a thumb at me.

"Really? This'll be fun," Amy's face lit up and she began looking at boxes, pulling some stuff out.

I looked at the shelves of clothes and shoes and frowned. It seemed frivolous. Didn't other people need this stuff?

"Are you sure?" I asked, quietly. "Nan already gave me a top and shorts."

"Yes, Prue," Hannah said, picking up on my reluctance. "Go nuts."

"You were never into clothes that much?" Amy asked. "Shopping?"

I shook my head. "Not really."

"Well, I'm sure we can pick out some stuff for you," Hannah laughed, and began looking through the shelves.

"Do you know your size?" Amy asked.

"No, I guess I've lost weight since…" Since I was living on the edge for three years. The air suddenly became thick.

"Yeah, you're a stick," Hannah exclaimed. She pulled out a few pairs of dark colored jeans and handed them to me. "Try these. You can change out back."

I escaped into the back room and lent against the wall, breathing hard. I was inside, in a walled town. They weren't here. They couldn't be. But, the images still flashed in my mind. I'd curled up inside a cupboard to hide and they'd scratched at the door trying to get in.

"How's the size?" Hannah called out, snapping me out of my near panic attack.

I quickly pulled on the jeans, but they were a little loose. "A little big."

"There's a smaller one there, try that."

"Okay."

This was too much. Too many things had changed. Too many people. Expectations. With a sigh, I tried on the smaller pair and they were a little firm. Pulling the shorts Nan had given me back on, I went out into the shop.

"Too small," I said, putting the jeans on the counter.

"Better take the larger one," Amy said.

"Yeah, Nan will no doubt feed you till you burst," Hannah agreed.

"I'll chuck a belt in for you, just incase."

I frowned at the pile they'd amassed while I was having a mini-breakdown. Tops, shirts, a warm looking jumper, a dark kaki colored coat, socks and even underwear.

"Did Shaw really carry you all that way?" Amy asked, folding the clothes into a box.

"I don't know," I shrugged. "I guess."

"He's single," Hannah winked.

I didn't like where this was going.

"He should take you out on a date."

"Where would they go?" Amy rolled her eyes.

I felt myself turning red when I thought about how he'd carried me six k's through the bush. And the fact I'd kicked him right between the legs. That was before he'd tried to save my life and right after he'd tried to shoot me.

"Here," Hannah flung something at me. "Take this. Is the size okay?"

A flimsy piece of black lace hit me in the chest and I realized she'd thrown a fancy bra at me and I turned red again.

"Hannah," Amy scolded.

"What?" she shrugged, smiling at me.

I'd only just met these girls and they were trying to set me up with Shaw? He'd saved me as a matter of consequence. He'd been there at the right time and it didn't mean that he was attracted to me. Did it?

The door opened then, letting in the afternoon sunshine, and I shoved the bra inside the pile of clothes.

"Afternoon, girls," came a female voice.

"Hi, Eva," Amy smiled brightly as I felt my stomach churn. This was the woman Hannah had warned me about and I caught her eye. She offered me a thin smile like she knew what was about to happen.

Taking a deep breath, I turned to face Eva and was greeted with the same impression I'd had earlier at the school. A do-gooder sort. Friendly school teacher turned snake in the grass. Pretty knee-length dress. Immaculate hair like she was some kind of Southern Belle, like Scarlett O'Hara from *Gone in the Wind*.

"You must be Prue," she declared, looking me over, a slight sneer pulling at her lip. I suddenly felt small and dirty. Exactly how she knew she made other people feel.

"Hello," I said to be polite, hoping she would go away.

"Welcome to our little town," she smiled brightly at me.

"Thanks."

"Are you getting some new clothes?" she asked, looking at the pile on the counter. "I hope my Dad gave you permission."

"Yes, he did," Hannah said, a sharp edge to her voice. "He said Prue could take whatever she wanted."

"I don't need it," I said, sensing a fight coming on. Eva and Hannah seemed to do this with a familiarity that put me on edge. I didn't want to be dragged into it.

"Prue, you need it," Hannah said firmly. "All your stuff was worn out. Mayor Thompson said you could."

I looked back at Eva who was regarding me with a smug expression. She knew she put me on edge. I bet she was counting on it.

"Well, don't take too much. There are other people who need it, too," she said haughtily.

"Don't be a bitch Eva," Hannah hissed at her.

"Excuse me?" she asked, crossing her arms over her chest.

"Prue's been through a lot. Not to mention she had a nasty accident. She doesn't need you coming in here being all high and mighty."

"Hannah Robertson," she scolded.

"I'm not one of your students, *Eva Thompson*," Hannah said. "If all you came here for was to be a bully, then you can just leave."

"Hannah," Amy hissed.

Eva let out an annoyed sigh and turned her gaze back onto me, looking up and down, her eyes lingering on my tattoos. "Well. All I came to do was say hello. It was nice to meet you, Prue. I'm sure we'll run into one another at some stage." And with that off her chest, she turned and left the shop, my mood suddenly at an all time low.

"She didn't want to say hello," Hannah screwed up her nose. "She wanted to check out the competition."

"Hannah, stop it," Amy shook her head. Turning to me, she said, "They've never got along."

"That's because she's a bitch and I don't make friends with bitches."

Somehow, I liked Hannah's point of view. I hoped I never crossed paths with Eva again, but the town was small and the likelihood of that happening was zero.

I dumped the rest of the clothes into the cardboard box, yanked it off the counter and said, "Thank you for the clothes."

"Prue," Hannah began, but I gave her a small smile and walked from the shop, the outside air enveloping me, lifting the weight that the enclosed space had been pushing on my shoulders.

"Are you okay?" She'd followed me out.

"It's just..."

"Too much?"

"Yeah."

"It's okay," she said kindly. "I get it. We all do. This is a different kind of life for you."

"I thought I was alone." It came out before I realized I was even thinking it.

"Here." Hannah took the box from me and set it on the footpath, then hugged me. It was such a strange sensation, I almost began sobbing my eyes out, but I held it in. I hadn't been hugged in a very long time and I was suddenly very grateful that Hannah Robertson had escaped the virus and ended up here.

When she pulled back she picked up the box and said, "C'mon. I'll walk with you back to Nan's."

"Okay."

As we walked the two blocks over, I couldn't help but feel that my earlier panic had been a little silly. I'd seen the town now and I understood that nothing was getting in. It couldn't. After all that time I'd spent wandering the waste alone, how could I feel safer out there where anything could get me?

At the end of the day, I wasn't sure how could a place like this could exist and how I hadn't found it earlier. It still felt like a dream.

Six

It was a nice feeling, not having to rely on crutches to get around. Without any stitches, it was unlikely that I'd tear the wound open again, so that meant I could go out and train at least a little. I kind of missed all the walking through the bush. It was my kind of normal. Screwed up, but normal.

Sifting through the bag of clothes Hannah and Amy had given me at the store, I found a pair of grey denim shorts. Short shorts, but I couldn't think of anything worse than trying to stretch my leg and exercise in trousers, so I dragged them on. I looked at the lacy underwear Hannah'd snuck into the pile and groaned. Like I'd need that, but I had to wear something.

One singlet, short shorts, combat boots and lacy bra later, I went out into the backyard with my sword under one arm. It was bright, still hot for this time of year, but there was a large tree at the back that shaded a large portion of the grassy yard. With my pale complexion, getting sunburnt would be the icing on the cake. Who needed a melanoma, right? As if I didn't have enough problems.

I looked at the jagged pinkish-red line that tore across my upper thigh and sighed. It split the tip of the dragon's tail clean in half. I'd gotten it tattooed five years ago, not long before I moved back to Australia. I'd been living in London at the time and that was a world gone. Now, life was more valuable than ruining a tattoo. I hadn't cared to look at them for a long time. I could tell you a story from them like a picture book. Now they were just a reminder of what was gone.

Twisting my hair back into a loose ponytail, I took a deep breath. I left the sword in the sheath, unclipping the leather strap and tested my leg with a few lunges and squats. It felt a little tight, but so far so good.

Closing my eyes, I listened to the sounds of the town, trying to find that calm place inside of me that I knew was there. It was strange being around life again and little reminders invaded my hearing. The slam of a door. The sound of a voice. I'd become so used to total silence, it felt loud and unnatural.

Drawing a deep breath, I raised the sword, leaning my weight to the left, onto the wounded leg. Practicing with the sword helped my balance. I used to go to the gym and punch the crap out of a bag, but that only helped with getting aggression out. Like MMA and any other martial art, balance and grace had a lot to do with inner strength. That's why I liked the sword. I had no idea if I was doing it properly, but I made up my own thing, remembering some of the kata moves I'd been taught.

It was like a graceful dance in a way, but using moves that could be turned into punches, kicks and blocks in a tight spot. I incorporated the sword not long after Quarantine to help keep my focus. A clear mind and a calm disposition were some of the things that had kept me alive for so long.

I'd been there for maybe half and hour when I felt someone watching me. I hadn't seen Shaw since the other day and when I caught sight of him spying on me, my heart did this little spasm in my chest. He was leaning against the side of the house watching me go through my made up kata and when he noticed that I'd found him out, he pushed off the wall, grinning.

"I hear you've been talking to everyone but me," he said, coming across the yard.

I nodded, noticing the way he'd jammed his hands into his pockets.

"What? No words of wisdom?"

It was a joke, but it kind of annoyed me. I just shook my head.

"What are you doing?"

I had to give him points for trying. *Again.* I pointed to my leg and the puckered red line and said, "Strength."

His lips curved into a smile when the third word I'd ever spoken to him came out of my mouth. "Yes. Prue. Strength. You chose your words carefully."

"To the point."

"Where do you learn how to do that?" he prodded, pointing to my sword.

I frowned at him and he laughed.

"What's Nan got you roped into?" he asked, changing the subject. "Knowing her, I assume she's lined something up for you to do."

"I'm helping with the milking."

"Well, you'll want to strengthen your back for that."

I shrugged. I supposed I would, but I'd just solider through it.

"Do you want to?" Shaw asked. "I mean, there are other things. The boys need help with the herd, sure, but you've got more useful skills."

"Like what?" My ears pricked up.

"You could help the guys who go out and scout. I'm positive they'd be into it."

I cocked my head to the side as if I'd asked him a question.

"We scout the entire area in sweeps over a week or so in every direction. We look for signs of movement in the area and to see if there's anything useful that can be scavenged."

"Oh."

"That's what I was doing when I found you."

"You tried to shoot me," I declared, scowling at him. He hadn't apologized for that yet.

"Whoa," he laughed, holding his hands up. "You're scary when you're angry, Prue."

"I have a sword, you know."

"Yeah." He ran a hand over his face, the shadow of stubble rasping against his skin. "I'm sorry about that. I didn't realize you were a woman *and* hurt."

I grimaced.

"The scope on that rifle is a piece of shit."

I didn't reply.

"But to make it fair, you did kick me in the balls."

I let out a surprised laugh, clapping a hand over my mouth. As if kicking him where it hurt equated with trying to shoot someone.

"Surprisingly good aim, too." He winced, then shifted on his feet. "You could always think about joining the guys on the wall when your legs a hundred percent."

"The wall?" I asked. Hannah had shown it to me yesterday on her tour.

"The wall is like a guard duty. We can't find everything out on a scout, so the wall guard is there to watch for any approach or looming threat. They also double as a fire watch in summer."

"Oh." That was kind of obvious now.

"Would you want to do something like that? It's all guys who do that kind of thing. Not because we're sexist or anything, it's just because none of the women want to do it."

"Maybe." I leant up against the fence that lined the yard, my fingers curling over the edge.

Shaw didn't look like he was in a hurry to be anywhere. He stood next to me and I could tell there were a million things he wanted to ask. His expression changed a few times before he came out with, "Where did you live before?"

"Ballarat."

He looked at my tattoos and said, "I bet you didn't get those there."

"No."

"Then where?"

I pointed to my arm. "I knew a guy in Melbourne." I pointed to my leg. "I knew a guy in London."

"You lived there? In London?"

"Yes."

"Why did you come back to Australia?"

I glanced sidelong at him, uncomfortable with all the questions.

"You don't have to tell me. I know I'm being a nosey bastard."

I'd lived in London for two years before everything went to shit. My boyfriend cheated on me. Left me for someone else. I was left alone and so heartbroken, I decided to come back to Australia. I'd been a broken, angry mess. Then the world ended and I was still a broken, angry mess.

I sighed. "It's a long story."

"Broken heart?" Shaw seemed to get it with an accuracy that infuriated me.

I shrugged. "Something like that."

"What's the story with the samurai sword?"

I set it down carefully against the fence next to me, the clink of metal reassuring. "It was my brother's."

"Oh," he said, looking away.

"His wife was from Japan. He collected them."

"What happened to them?"

I knew he didn't mean the swords. I shrugged. I don't know what happened to them.

"You parents?"

"When I left, they were already sick."

"I'm sorry."

"It's not your fault."

Shaw looked like he wanted to reach out and touch me, but he must have thought better of it and his hand dropped to his side, clutching the edge of the fence.

What use was there telling my little sob story? His was probably the same. Everyone got sick and died. Everyone who wasn't sick died of other things. Shaw's family probably got sick as well. Everyone's family got sick.

"My Dad was a commanding officer in the Army," he said, suddenly. "My Mum died a few years before. He didn't get sick. He got shot in the head trying to do the right thing. Trying to help people. I might be a bastard for saying so, but I'm glad my Mum died before this happened. I'm glad she didn't have to live through this."

I don't know why, but I reached over and put my hand on his. Instantly, I regretted it when I saw the hungry look in his eyes. I dropped my hand away abruptly and picked up my sword.

"Shaw?" The annoying and unmistakable trill of Eva's voice floated across the yard.

He tried to mask whatever expression flashed across his face before calling out, "Yeah?"

Her blonde head appeared around the side of the house and she started when she saw me, but quickly smiled. "Dad asked me to come find you. He wants a word."

"Okay," he sighed, clearly annoyed. "I'll be there in a minute."

She stood there waiting and he turned to me, suddenly unsure of what to say. I caught the smug expression on Eva's face out the corner of my eye and did them both a favor. I backed away and walked across the yard and into the house, not looking back.

"She's a jealous little bitch, if you ask me," Hannah proclaimed, picking up another chicken egg and putting it into her already too full basket.

I had escaped the confines of Nan's as much for something to do as to escape my traitorous thoughts. Helping Hannah collect eggs from the smelly chicken coup was better than nothing. It was easy on my leg and the bending was good exercise for my disused muscles.

"What do you mean?" I asked, feigning confusion.

"Eva Thompson has had her eye on Shaw since day one." She almost dropped the top layer of eggs on the ground. "If she hasn't got him by now, she never will."

"I don't like him like that." Like I cared.

Hannah shrugged, "If you say so."

I glared at her and bent down to collect a few more eggs.

"All I'm saying is, the man saved your life and he's been following you around like a lost puppy dog. If you don't like him, he definitely likes you."

Following me around? He'd only come to see how I was doing a few times. That could hardly be seen as following.

Why the hell would he want to follow me? Even if I was different and new, he'd soon lose interest.

"Welcome back to high school," she laughed. "The rumor mill works pretty well around here. Better get used to it."

"I don't know anything about anything."

"Thatta girl!"

We left the chicken coop and I fastened the door behind me. Hannah had explained that one coop they kept for breeding and the other they kept to collect eggs from. When the population of chickens became high enough, they would slaughter the elders for their meat and feathers, and let the younger ones take their place and introduce new hens into the 'egg stock'.

Their biggest problem was having enough to go around so everyone had a balanced diet. Red meat was scarce, but sometimes the guards on the wall would spot kangaroos and scouts would go out and hunt and bring something back. I could relate to that, having had a lot of trouble finding food in the early days.

"I'm glad I met you, Prue," Hannah said suddenly. "You mightn't say much, but you're a lot more practical than the other women here. You're strong and independent and I bet you could beat the shit outta all the guys too. Twice a day and three times on Sunday! It's good to finally have someone to talk to who gets it."

I peered at her curiously. "Thanks."

"We were all pretty lucky when everything went down," she continued. "Brian, the mayor, he got everyone together and they built the town into what you see now. Most of the people here are locals. They never had a hard day in their lives. This," she gestured around us, "this is as hard as it got for them. They don't know what survival means, not like you."

No, I bet they didn't.

"You're starting with the boys down the milking shed tomorrow?" Hannah asked, thankfully changing the subject.

"Yes."

"Look out for Paul," she winked. "He's a good guy, but he likes to play pranks. Check your stool before you sit down. Actually, check everything before you sit on it or pick it up."

"Okay," I smiled.

"They won't give you shit, Prue. They're okay, but they might put it on your stuff."

Nice to see that some people hadn't lost their sense of humor. I helped Hannah carry the baskets up to the shop where we left them with Amy and another older woman I hadn't met before, Sarah. And since Hannah lived three streets over from Nan's we walked together through the town. I wanted to get back in time to help Nan with dinner and anything she needed. I felt useless, not doing anything. I wasn't used to all this idle time and it was doing my head in.

"Oh, look out," Hannah said suddenly, the amusement in her voice giving away who she'd seen. "What was I telling you before?"

Looking up, I saw Shaw walking towards us, his hands jammed into the pockets of his trousers again. Maybe he was following me around like a lost puppy dog. Or maybe he was just being friendly to the girl he'd almost shot.

"Hey, Shaw," Hannah called out.

"Hey," came his now familiar voice.

"I'll catch you later, Prue," she said to me with a wink and I realized she was going to ditch me. "If you wanna help tomorrow, I'll be round Doc's at eight."

"Okay," I said, grimacing at her.

She laughed at my reaction and waved to Shaw as she took off down the footpath.

"Twice in one day?" I said when he stopped in front of me.

"Are you going back to Nan's?" he asked and when I nodded he continued, "I'll walk you then."

"I'm sure I'll be okay."

"Prue. Let me walk you."

I just walked off. A moment later he was beside me again.

"Did you help Hannah with the chooks?" he asked, though it sounded like he was trying to find another excuse to get me talking again.

"Yes."

"Fun?"

"Thrilling."

"What did you do before? For work?"

"Lots of things." I'd been one of those people who was never satisfied with one job. A year would go by and I'd start getting restless and I'd quit and look for something else. I'd done a lot of different things.

"Like what?" Shaw asked. "What was the last job you had?"

Well, that was depressing. "I stacked shelves in a

supermarket."

"Nothing wrong with that," he said. "Do whatever, I say. As long as it makes you happy."

"I didn't like people."

"Customer Service wasn't a strength, huh?"

"No," I shook my head. "You?"

"Defense Force," he said wryly.

Defense Force didn't always mean being a soldier. "Were you in the army? Like your Dad?"

"Yeah. I was training for the SAS right before, you know. But, before that I was infantry. Sniper." I knew enough to know that SAS meant Special Forces.

"Figures," I said, remembering his rifle.

He laughed, picking up on the reference. How couldn't he? "We were taught basic hand to hand and self defense, but they had a stronger focus on weapons techniques. I obviously did a lot of marksman training."

"Still a shit shot."

"Prue," he scolded. "Luckily for you."

I grimaced and shook my head. Stop joking about it. It wasn't funny. Instead I asked, "What's your first name?"

"Andrew."

I screwed up my face. It didn't suit him.

"What?" he laughed.

"You don't look like an Andrew."

"You don't look like a Prudence," he retorted.

I just rolled my eyes and kept walking, much to his

amusement. I was surprised at how comfortable Shaw made me feel after everything. All that time not trusting anyone, hiding, running... I'd spoken to him three times since he brought me here and I felt like I'd known him longer. All those carefully placed defense mechanisms had just crumbled. It wasn't only him. It was everyone I'd met so far. Well, except for Eva Thompson.

Shaw coughed nervously and I was a little surprised. He was nervous? I made him nervous? I suppose so. I was a little unpredictable.

"You never told me what you were doing this morning," he said after a minute.

"Kata," I said. "For calm. Strength." I pointed to my leg.

"You did a lot of martial arts?"

"I was a very angry person," I shrugged. "I did a lot of stuff. It helps."

"Like what?"

I knew he was just trying to prolong the conversation and I wasn't keen on talking about before all that much. "Boxing, MMA, swimming, archery." Violence was my coping mechanism. Not a very healthy one, but it came in handy after the world fell apart. "Anger management." I shrugged it off.

Shaw seemed to get that he was getting closer to me talking about my time alone and he hesitated. "Out there?" he asked quietly, rubbing his palms on his trousers.

"There aren't any rules."

We stood out the front of Nan's, the rose bushes rocking slightly in the breeze and I tried to cram down the memories that had begun to rush to the surface. Memories

I'd hoped I'd forget with time.

"Did you ever go back home?" Shaw asked and I felt my breath catch.

How could I explain it? The horror of the burnt. The destruction. Them. He was looking at me expectantly, so I nodded.

"And?"

My eyes fell to the ground and I shook my head, taking a step back. And what? Did he really want to know or was this some kind of twisted way to get me talking? As if talking would make things better. You can't see death like that and forget. Things like that followed a person to the grave.

Shaw didn't make a move to press for more, so I turned and walked away.

No one needed to know about that.

I must have sat there for hours watching the roadblock.

Barriers were strung across the breadth of the road, right across the nature strips either side. A dark green tent was on one side and one of those huge army jeeps was parked across from it. Orange reflectors were spaced out across the barricade and flashed every now and then. Must have some kind of solar charge in them.

Ever since I'd hidden myself under the bush in the mud at the side of the highway, nothing had moved. Nothing but trash strewn about by the wind. The occasional sparrow landed on the barricade or the jeep, but nothing human came or went.

In the distance, maybe about a kilometer away, I could make out the Arch of Victory. It was a huge stone arch that spanned the entire road. It had been built as a war memorial, the trees that lined the highway each bore a plaque for every fallen soldier in every World War that had lived in the area. But, there was no one left to remember them. That much was clear from my silent vigil on the road block ahead.

I'd had to walk through the housing development to get here, or what was left of it. Whole blocks of newly built houses were burnt out and destroyed, any sign of the people who'd once lived here was long gone.

Three months. It had all fallen apart in less than three months. The thought of what had happened made me sick. The lengths the government had gone to to contain the virus and the people left over. They were all gone. Anyone who'd remained in the town had been rounded up. Sick or no.

The day was fast fading into late afternoon, so I when I was satisfied that no one was here, I shimmied out of my hiding place and made my way down the footpath towards the road block.

As I crossed the barricade, my suspicions were confirmed. It was deserted.

Looking into the jeep, I jerked back in surprise when I saw the shape of a person inside. When no sound came, I looked back through the glass and almost threw up. The opposite door was wide open and the remains of whoever the person had been, was pulled half out of the drivers seat and was half something else. Eaten. I'd seen some horrible things and done some of them too, but that was just *wrong*.

Backing away quickly, I kept going, passing underneath the Arch, watching and listening for anything out of the ordinary. Remembering that there was a supermarket a block away, I made a beeline for it, hoping that something edible was still there.

I kind of expected the place to be trashed and I was right. Windows were smashed, stuff was littered everywhere in the car park. There was even the burnt out shell of a car and several shopping trolleys. Poking my head through a smashed window, I realized that I was wasting my time looking here. Every single shelf was bare, the rancid small of frozen food gone bad stuck in my nose and made me gag. It was dark and menacing, the further the shop went back and the thought of poking around in there scared the hell out of me. Even if I was hungry.

That night I barricaded myself into a house that overlooked the road. Watching the darkness was eerie. You get used to having your life lit up, no matter what time it was and to see a residential street this dark and devoid of life, it made my whole body tingle. It wasn't right, but it was reality. That whole day, I'd seen nothing. I was instantly reminded of that movie *I am Legend*. It was exactly like that. Overgrown gardens, cracked roads, smashed up buildings. The remains of human life slowly being taken back by nature. All that was missing were the vampires.

I sat in the window, hidden by the curtains and watched for any movement. Out of habit more than anything, but who knew what would come out under the cover of darkness. If I caught sight of an animal, I'd try and trap it. Or if I caught sight of another wanderer like me, I'd be better off knowing where they went before they knew about me.

In reality, I hoped I wouldn't see anything. The more alone I was, the safer I was.

That's when I saw the outline of a person walking down the center of the street. My breath caught as I watched their movements and I realized something was different. They were moving slow, their movements jerky, like they had been sapped of energy or had a dislocated shoulder. My mind instantly made the connection with zombie, but as the light caught their face, I knew that wasn't it. It had been a man. I could see the masculinity in its features, but all his hair had fallen out and his skin was spread taught over his skull. It was like all the muscle and fat had dropped away and all that was left was a skeleton encased in skin.

It was nothing like the walking dead from television and movies. This was something else entirely. As it continued prowling, it let out a strange clicking sound from the back of it's throat and every few steps, a whistle like some kind of macabre whale song. I don't know who it was talking to, it was the only one I could see.

What the hell should I do now? What if it could smell me? What if it wanted to eat me? My gut twisted in fear and I swallowed hard. I shouldn't have come here.

It's head shot up and I stumbled to my feet, grasping my sword. It was looking straight at me. It lumbered towards the front door of the house, slow but purposeful, like it was on a mission. Then I remembered the person in the jeep.

A split second later, it was if it had come alive and it was scraping at the front door and I could either run or hide. I had nothing inside of me then but fear. My heart thudded with it and my hands shook. I couldn't stand and fight. The door knob began to turn as the creature seemed to work out how to get in and I cursed to myself for not barricading it.

Silently moving into the kitchen, I opened the cabinet under the sink and breathed a little sigh of relief that it was one of those continuous ones that was open the entire length of the wall. I had no time to think about it. I slid my small body into the tiny space and closed the door behind me, the latch clicking into place.

I huddled closer in the cabinet and tried to still my breathing. Fear paralyzed me as I heard the thump of footsteps crossing the kitchen floor. When they stopped right in front of where I was hiding, my eyes widened and I steeled myself for the inevitable.

Then, there was sniffing at the door. Sharp blows of air, like an animal foraging for food, then nothing. I knew better than to make a move and a minute later there was a thud against the wood right next to my head and the whole cabinet shuddered. I swallowed hard, trying to fight the blind fear that was pulsing through every inch of my body. Stay still. Don't move. Don't give yourself away.

The thing made a low whistling sound and the thump of footsteps went back along the kitchen floor, receding into the next room. I clutched my fingers around the hilt of my sword, praying to god that it wouldn't come back. Somehow, I think my saving grace was the fact that the kitchen was stuck in the seventies. The latches were press button. Whatever that thing had been, it mustn't have the brain capacity to know to push in the latch to open the door. And that had just saved my life.

Everything inside me told me to stay put until morning and

even if I had the guts, I wouldn't have got out for anything. Whatever that thing had been, it had once been human. Was it a zombie? A vampire like in that movie? Somehow I didn't think so. Maybe the virus didn't kill everyone, but mutated those who survived? I didn't want to know. The thought was too terrifying to handle.

If there was one thing movies and books had taught me about creatures that wandered the night looking for food, it was to keep out of dark places during the day. I was suddenly very glad that I'd passed on going into that supermarket.

When daylight finally crept through the cracks of my hiding place, I ran from the remains of civilization and never looked back.

Home was gone.

Seven

For the next few weeks, I tried my best to fall into a routine. That meant letting go of some of my insecurities and habits, though they would never be forgotten.

It took me a while to get the hang of milking the cows. I'd do one to the boys' twenty and no amount of help made me understand the proper way. Apparently there was a right angle, but it took me ages to get it, but when I did, I managed to catch up the pace. Now with my help it took almost two hours off their total milking time.

Every morning I'd get up at five am and walk down to the sheds for six thirty, but I was always early. Paul usually let the cattle into the shed by the time we got there, but I'd taken it upon myself to help him.

This morning I'd slept a little later than usual, but since I was still technically early, I didn't rush. I liked the walk through town in the mornings. Actually, I savored it. The quiet calm before everyone got up, though most people seemed to rise with the sun anyway, and the sense of security. I could walk and let my mind wander, luxuries I hadn't had in a long time.

"Prue!"

I turned when I heard Shaw calling out to me. Over the last few weeks, I'd seen him every so often. He'd come over to train with me when he could and no matter what I did, he never seemed put off from coming back. I'd taught him some kata and he'd taught me some of the hand-to-hand that he'd learnt in the army. I'd spent long hours in the gym before when I'd had nothing to do and touching sweaty guys didn't get to me like it did with Shaw. Usually, I'd be beating them into a pulp, but Shaw seemed to use it as an excuse to touch me. And I'd catch myself looking at him in *that* way and I swear he'd noticed more than once, but he never said anything.

Right now, he thumped down the stairs of the Mayor's house and crossed the yard to come meet me. "You're late today."

"It's six thirty," I said, my eye catching a smug looking Eva on the porch. My gaze travelled to his hair, which looked shorter.

He shrugged like it was no big deal. "Eva just cut it for me."

Eva smiled sweetly at me over Shaw's shoulder. She was cutting Shaw's hair at six thirty in the morning? That stunk of something I didn't want to think about.

I took in her smug expression and decided it wasn't worth it. She wanted a reaction. "Well," I said in my quiet voice. "She did a good job."

The smirk fell from her face and I turned and kept walking towards the pens at the opposite side of town. The boys would be waiting for me and I'd lingered too long already.

"Shaw?" Eva's voice was louder than it needed to be.

"I've gotta go to the wall, Eva. Sorry."

I kept walking and didn't look back. What did I have to be jealous of? The fact that love could still exist in the shit hole the world had become was a joke. Let the selfish little bitch have the handsome ex-army sniper. Whatever.

Maybe he just went over for breakfast with the Mayor? Maybe he was with Eva? So what. What business was it of mine? A little voice said, *he never told you about her all those times he put his arms around you.* I shook my head as I rounded the corner out of sight. That was just training. It wasn't anything else.

I was never the most popular kid at school. I was awkward and shy and kids who wanted to feel better about their own shit lives used me to make themselves feel big. I became good at avoiding people and existing inside myself. A skill that became very useful for another kind of survival. Now I was back among people and still didn't know how to function properly.

I just wanted to shrink and be as small as possible because if they couldn't see me, then I wouldn't be a target.

I pushed my way into the cow shed and grabbed a bucket and stool. Greg was milking a heifer at the back and stood when he heard me banging about.

"Prue," he called. "I've already done the back two, can you start from that end? We'll meet in the middle." He didn't ask why I was late and I wondered how much longer I could go on doing this. What did they have to complain about? I put my head down and I worked. I contributed just like Mayor Thompson asked me to. Of an afternoon, I even went and helped Nan with whatever she needed.

But deep down, I wished my leg would get better. It didn't sit well with me being so feeble. Milking cows. Washing and sewing. Making jam. I wanted to go back to the waste. It sounded like a perverted case of Stockholm Syndrome. Even though it was screwed up, it was what I knew and people felt most comfortable with what they knew.

I slammed down a barrier between my thoughts and the task at hand, a technique I'd used on many occasions to keep going and set about milking my share of the heifers. Some things didn't bare thinking about anymore.

"Are you okay?" Paul asked, rounding the back of the cow I was currently milking. He was probably about thirty years old, but he'd grown in a thick black beard that made him look closer to forty. Paired with the town's trademark flannel shirt and work boots, he looked like a cross between a lumberjack and a farmer out of a children's book. All he needed were the suspenders.

"Yes," I said, not looking up, focusing on each spray of milk into the bucket.

"You seem more abrupt than usual," he said. "Did you and Shaw have a barney?"

I hesitated. Not because he seemed to think Shaw and I were an item, but the way he asked it reminded me of my Dad. Instead of coming out and saying it plainly, 'did you have a fight?', he'd lay it on thick with the slang. It was all a ruse to get me laughing, of course and it'd work every time. Especially when he called me a 'flamin' galah'.

"No. We're okay." I went back to milking. It was the illustrious Eva 'Perfect' Thompson who always seemed to be there to stick a thorn in my side.

"Okay," Paul said after a minute. "But, careful on Bessy's udder. You'll rip her teat right off."

I couldn't help looking up and smiling.

"That's better." He patted Bessy on the rump and wandered off down the line. How he knew which cow was which was beyond me. They all looked exactly the same.

Shaw and Eva. Eva and Shaw. How I kept letting it get to me was one of the great mysteries of the universe. After everything, shouldn't I be the woman of steel? I rested my cheek against Bessy's warm flank and she shifted in the hay, turning her head towards me. I watched as she chewed on a mouthful of food, long pieces of grass and hay sticking out of her mouth.

Life must be so simple for a cow. Only having to worry about sleeping and eating, being protected from harm. If only things were that simple for me.

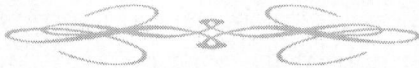

"Hello, Prue," a cheery voice trilled behind me.

I turned around, stifling a sigh as Eva Thompson stopped by me on the footpath. I was on my way from the farm back to Nan's and still wasn't over this mornings little haircut incident. The last thing I wasted was to have a conversation with sweetness and light herself.

"We haven't really gotten a chance to talk." She smiled sweetly and I look in her bright floral dress and perfectly combed blonde hair. She seemed totally out of place in this world, but I could see why she was appointed the school teacher. Eva Thompson could turn it on and off with the flick of a switch. She could make a scary story instill as much fear as a nursery rhyme.

"Last week at the shop," she continued, "it wasn't a really good introduction. I'm really protective over everyone in the town and that thing with Hannah..." she sighed and flipped her hair back over her shoulder, "Hannah and I have never seen eye to eye."

I wondered why that was.

"All I'm saying is that you're welcome here." As welcome as her need to hear me reply, it seemed. "It's great that Shaw rescued you and all, Prue, but don't let it get to you."

"Why?" I asked, not really wanting to hear the inevitable.

"Oh my," she exclaimed, a look of exaggerated pity in her eyes. "Do you think he has feelings for you?"

"I never said…"

"Shaw is a nice guy. I mean, he's just looking out for you like we all are. We all want to see you settle in and heal, but don't think too much of it. With the way the world is now, we all have to look out for one another, but it doesn't mean that we fall in love every single time someone does something nice for us."

I scowled, brushing my hair behind my ear. There might not be high schools anymore, but this was playground bullying. Eva was the mean girl and I was the science geek and she'd just dumped the preverbal milkshake over my head. By the end of the day the whole school would be talking about me behind my back. I guess I was twenty-seven, but right now I felt like a fourteen year old with a stupid crush on a popular boy.

"It's okay, Prue," Eva took my hand and it was all I could do not to visibly cringe. "I understand. After everything you've been through it's natural to want to latch onto the person who saved you from certain death."

What the hell would she know about it?

"I'm here for you, okay? I just don't want to see your heart broken when you realize Shaw and I..." She smiled, dropping my hand. "Well, you know. Anyway-" She bounced on the balls of her feet, suddenly chipper. "I've promised to run some errands for Dad, so I better hop to it. Take care, Prue."

And with that she waved, flipping her blonde hair as she twirled around and almost skipped down the footpath in the opposite direction like she was some kind of Snow White on acid. I was seriously beginning to think that someone had slipped me something, but the embarrassment that ate at my heart was all to real.

I stormed across the street, head down and face burning. It was official. I hated Eva Thompson with the fire of a thousand suns. I hoped mutants would come and eat her. Scratch that. That was something too horrible to wish on anyone, even my worst enemy. I just hoped she'd get as good as she gave so she'd know how it felt.

"Prue?"

My head snapped up at the sound of my name and I came face to face with Greg, who I'd almost walked past without noticing.

"Is everything okay? I saw you talking with Eva. Actually, I should say Eva was talking at you."

"I'm fine," I said.

"Here," he gestured for me to follow him, "come sit down a minute."

He led me over to the park and sat on the bench next to the footpath. I didn't have it in me to decline and Greg had been nothing but nice to me, even when I got frustrated trying to get the hang of milking. "Eva's just got her knickers in a twist because Shaw pays attention to you."

I sighed, sitting down next to him.

"Do you have feelings for him?"

I could neither confirm or deny that, so I didn't say anything.

"It's understandable if you do," Greg continued. "I mean, he did save your life and all."

"It doesn't mean anything, Greg," I said, cutting him off.

Raising and eyebrow he shrugged. "It means a hell of a lot. People do some fucked up things to save someone. I know all about it."

It was like he was reading my mind, except the only person I was saving was myself.

"Listen," he said when I wasn't forthcoming. "Don't worry about Eva. She can be a right bitch sometimes, but she hasn't got some kind of hold over Shaw or anything. If she hasn't won him over by now, then she probably never will."

Hannah had said the same thing. Everyone was worked up over a potential match between Shaw and I to even notice the fact that Eva's bullying could break apart my facade. The facade that said everything inside me was okay. If she kept chipping away, then maybe I'd have to be left out in the bush again or put into a straight jacket.

"I'm not worried about Shaw," I said, looking out over the

empty street.

Greg shifted nervously beside me, kicking the toe of his boot into the dry ground. I stood and began to walk down the footpath.

"Hey, Prue, I didn't mean…" he called out after me, but I held up a hand in a wave and kept walking.

"See you tomorrow."

Eight

I arced my sheathed sword through the afternoon air, holding in my stomach and concentrating on my balance. As I turned at the waist, my eyes collided with Shaw's. It still got to me, how oddly green they were and in the sunlight the irises were iridescent like glass.

It began like this almost every day for the last few weeks. I'd be out in Nan's yard after getting back from milking and five minutes later, Shaw would turn up without a word and just join in. Not every day, he had his shifts to do on the wall, but whenever he was free he'd just be *there*. At first I was annoyed, but it had fast become the norm and I didn't pay him any attention anymore. I had no idea what his game was, but I wasn't playing it. Not when it put me into the firing line with a certain blonde snake.

Now that we knew more about each other's routines, we just went through the motions. Warming up, strength training and the fun part. Beating his ass.

No weapons were allowed. It was just me and him and that

was all the more satisfying, knowing that I could put him on his back being as tiny as I was. He stood a head over me and had a definite weight advantage, but that meant nothing when you could anchor yourself in the right place.

Not long into our session it was glaringly obvious that today I was off my game. All I could think about was yesterday and every time Shaw's skin would come into contact with mine, I would falter. Every block, punch and kick jarred through me like lightning.

Shaw was just as surprised as I was when he slipped around and grabbed me from behind, pinning my arms to my sides, our breathing labored. Every single place he touched me was on fire and in our current position, I could feel all of him against my back. And I meant *all* of him.

"Prue?" he whispered in my ear, breath tickling my neck.

I didn't know what to do. Formulating a response wasn't happening and that's when I felt his lips against the skin of my neck. At least, I thought it was. The sensation was so light, I could have been dreaming. Every single one of Eva's words from the day before flashed through my mind and the result wasn't good. Before he could get any ideas, I kicked my leg through the middle of his and hooked my foot around his shin, taking his knee from under him. The tension on my arms loosened and I grabbed him under the shoulder, using my weight to flip him forward. Basic self-defense for women one-oh-one.

Shaw landed on his back with a grunt, staring up at the sky in surprise.

"Wow," he said. "Just…wow."

He looked up at me, squinting his eyes in the sunshine and I shrugged. "What did you expect?"

"I think that's enough for today," he said, sitting up. "Why do all of these sessions always end with my ass on the ground?"

"You need to pay more attention." Obviously.

Running a hand through his hair, he laughed. On his feet a second later, he grabbed his bottle of water. "See you tomorrow."

"Bye." I watched as he rounded the corner of the house, disappearing from sight, but still firmly planted everywhere else. Of course I had feelings for him. I'd be stupid not to admit it, but the truth was that Shaw treated me like I mattered. More than any guy had ever done before and after Quarantine. He kept me stuck together.

My story wasn't about falling in love. My story was about not falling apart.

One thought went through my mind that night and all the next day while milking. Shaw's lips on my neck.

I tossed and turned in bed all night until the point I had to get up and dump the quilt and pillow on the floor. Only with the hard boards underneath my back could I drift off and it was headfirst into dreams with dirty undertones. And all of a sudden, there I was coming in my sleep like a pubescent teenager. The thought of Shaw... Washing with a bucket of cold water never felt so good.

And milking. Milking brought up a whole new kind of flush and now I was glad to get out of there and into some fresh air. Another training session and I thought I might break.

On the walk back to Nan's, I found myself passing the old post office that housed the school. I lingered on the footpath a moment, looking at the empty playground. The sounds of someone playing a guitar drifted from the open doors of the classroom and it made my spine tingle. Life seemed to find a way to go on, no matter what. It was unsettling in a way.

Hannah had told me, back on that first day she'd taken me on the unofficial tour, that there were seven kids of various ages in the town and even a little baby.

It was a strange thing to see children running around again and it made me wonder what kind of future they could have. If there were other places like this, would they ever find them? Would they have the chance to fall in love and have children of their own? The way things were now, it didn't look like a possibility and I wondered if they understood what had happened. But, I guess they didn't know the difference.

"Hey." I turned at the sound of a familiar voice and saw Shaw walking towards me. He always seemed to pop up when I was feeling vulnerable and hot for him. A trait I found absolutely infuriating.

Eva chose that moment to walk out into the yard all smiles and sunshine ushering the kids outside for their recess. She caught sight of Shaw and I standing by the fence and she raised a hand and waved. I didn't move. She wasn't waving at me.

She smiled brightly and I couldn't help but feel a little sick. Eva was beautiful and a sweet school teacher, real marriage material. They were made for each other. Eva and Shaw.

Shaw and Eva.

Shaw snorted and waved back, which took me a little by surprise. "I'm due to go out tomorrow," he said like he regretted it. "I'll be gone a week."

"Okay." I didn't need a play by play.

"Before I go, I should introduce you to Captain Wallis. You'd be good on the wall. Out there." He squinted his eyes against the sun, looking away.

Maybe he thought I wouldn't want to go back. "I'd like that."

"Good." When he smiled his whole face changed. In a good way. "Later then."

I nodded, suddenly hopeful that something more interesting than milking cows had presented itself. "Later."

"I'll come by Nan's after dinner?"

"Sure."

I watched him walk away down the footpath and I wasn't quite sure what to feel. Excited about the possibility of doing something more? Working the wall and maybe going out on my own again. The thought crossed my mind that maybe this Captain Wallis would ask me to go out into the bush with Shaw. Then what would I do? Shit, what would *he* do?

All those times we'd hung out, he'd never once asked me about before or after. Not since the day after Doc took out my stitches. Without all of that, we didn't have that much to talk about. His life seemed to be tied up with the waste just as much as mine was.

Sighing, I looked back up at the playground and Eva caught my eye. She smiled, but it was half-hearted. Avoiding the

Mayor's daughter had worked out well enough so far, but it only worked when she wasn't trying to seek me out to sink her claws in. I smiled back just as enthusiastically and walked the opposite direction towards Nan's before she could formulate a scheme in her pretty blonde head.

The man in charge of the wall was named Graham Wallis, but everyone called him Captain. He was one of the few people in charge that I hadn't met yet and he was all smiles when Shaw took me round his house.

Amy greeted me with a huge smile and a hug. Catching Shaw's eye over her shoulder he stifled a laugh at my wide eyed expression.

"It's nice to finally meet you, Prue," Captain said, gesturing for us to sit on the couch, while he took an armchair that looked well worn.

"Thank you."

"Shaw tells me that he thinks you'd be good on the wall."

"Yes."

"We could use the extra hands," Shaw put in.

"Extra hands are always needed everywhere," Captain lamented. "But, we'd be grateful to have you."

"Thanks," I said with a small smile.

"We'd put you on the wall first. It's more like border protection," he explained. "No doubt you've seen some things out there and understand what I mean."

I nodded. I'd seen just about everything.

"We like to know if anyone's coming, or if something has changed. And especially if anything can be scavenged. We're always in need of spare parts or just ordinary day to day things. Clothing, material, medicine."

I frowned. Medicine? That was a long shot and the thought of going into town to search a hospital made my heart thump painfully.

"Is something wrong?" Captain asked, his eyes shifting to Shaw.

"No, I..." I didn't know how to say it. Don't go into town. That would have been a start. But the thought of how many things would be hanging around in a hospital made me weak in the knees and I was sitting down.

"We know going to a city is a long shot," Shaw said as if he'd sensed my fear. "Three years is a long time to hope that anything useful might be left."

"We could always use an extra hand on the wall," Captain continued. "We're spread pretty thin. We don't expect you to go back out, not if you don't want to, but your knowledge would be invaluable. Your self-defense and survival skills."

I wondered why they hadn't asked me earlier, but I guess they wanted to wait until I was adjusted enough. Trouble was, I didn't think I would ever feel at peace again.

"Yes," I said. "I would like to help if I can."

"Okay. We won't ask you to go overboard, but somehow I think you'll have no trouble keeping up with those louts," Captain smiled. "I understand you already know Bobby, so I'll pair you up with him for a few days. Just tell me when you want to start."

"Tomorrow."

"Are you sure the boys down the farm won't be sore about it?"

"Of course they'll be sore," Shaw laughed.

Captain shook his head with a grin. "Six am start. You okay with that?"

"Yes." It wasn't a change from what I was already doing.

"Beautiful," he clapped his hands together. "I'll be down the gate early to let Shaw out, so just meet us there."

I nodded, offering a smile. This was infinitely more exciting than milking cows, but I didn't count on the fact that I'd have to watch Shaw leave. I'd become used to his presence, no matter how annoying he was. I'd actually miss him and I wasn't sure how to deal with it. Becoming close to people opened me up to the one thing I didn't want to feel again. The pain of losing them.

The next day, I went to the gate as promised and Captain paired me up with Bobby, the guy I now knew Hannah had a crush on, and they let Shaw out as scheduled. I watched him from the top of the wall as he disappeared into the surrounding bush, his pack on his back and that rifle I'd had a close encounter with over one shoulder. A new emotion coursed through me then and I squashed it down.

"He'll be fine," Bobby said and I wondered if everyone thought he and I were a secret item.

"I know."

And with that, I settled into a new routine. Walking the wall. Buddying with Bobby for a few days as a kind of training program. It was a lot of watching and waiting and nothing exciting. Now that I had the opportunity to look out on the remains of the world, it really felt like we were truly alone.

With Shaw gone it was quiet. Nan kept me busy when I wasn't on the wall, churning out cheese and jam like nobody's business. Hannah did her best to drive me to distraction and even tried to train with me one day, but gave up after ten minutes and sat on the back porch in the shade, watching. They all seemed to pick up on my lack of enthusiasm with the absence of one particular ex-army sniper. I tried to shrug it off, but I couldn't help but worry about him out there all alone. I knew exactly what it was like and that was the problem.

So, that's how Amy found us. In Nan's backyard, me running through a kata and Hannah in the shade, a steamy Mills&Boon romance book in her hand. And when I saw the look on Amy's face, I knew that Shaw was back.

"Hey, Prue," she called. "Dad wants to see you if you've got a minute. Shaw's back."

My face must have fell, because she waved a hand. "No, nothing's wrong. He wants to ask you a favor."

A favor from me? That could only mean one thing.

He wanted me to go out into the waste with Shaw.

Nine

Being out in the waste was familiar, yet strange. After the weeks spent in the town, it almost felt alien. Being alone and having Shaw walk beside me was even weirder. As I'd expected, Captain asked me to go out on a scout and I'd agreed. I don't know why, but the thought of Shaw out here on his own… He'd done it a million times, but I still didn't like it. And a week later, here we were in the middle of the waste, day one of our little road trip.

Shaw didn't really need to explain to me what he did out here. It was plain for anyone to see, but he gave me the speech anyway. As we walked through the bush, he spoke softly, telling me about his week long trips and what exactly he did out here on his own.

It was as Captain Wallis said. Scavenging, watching, that kind of thing. Like a border protection detail. Shaw had a map that he used to point out his route to me. He'd change it up every so often, each time going another direction, or a little further. We were going north-east across a lot of flat country that was once used for cattle grazing and canola crops. There were a few small towns marked on the map, but he said he kept away from them. They'd been picked clean of anything useful a long time ago.

Towards midday we came across a small farmhouse. Shaw approached it with such familiarity, I knew he came here a lot. His hand came up, shielding his eyes from the sun and he scanned the yard and the house. I waited a little awkwardly. He was meant to be showing me what he did out here, wasn't he? I wasn't really used to being the apprentice of my own life.

After a moment he seemed satisfied that nothing had changed and I followed him round back, where he began to climb up onto the roof. I watched the path he took and mimicked it, carefully placing my feet and hands where he had placed his. The way he knew the safest path up to the roof meant he used this method of surveying often. I grasped his outstretched hand and he hauled me up the last section, onto the main part of the house.

The roof was clad in corrugated iron and it had become hot in the sun. Shaw sat underneath the eave in the shade and began to scan the horizon.

"It's so flat out this way, it's the only way to see any good distance," he shrugged as I sat next to him.

My bare leg bumped against his and I pulled back, trying to be casual about it, but I'm sure it didn't come off like that. I turned my head away, scanning the countryside to the left. It was strange how comfortable I had become with Shaw after everything, but I still didn't like him touching me, even during our training sessions. When my leg bumped his, it was like a god damn romance novel. I didn't need that shit, especially not out here.

"We alter the pattern every time, incase someone's watching." Shaw's voice was loud in the silence.

I looked back and found him staring, his gaze lingering on my thigh. I raised an eyebrow and said, "What do you look for?" Even though I already knew the answer.

He looked back out across the flats, hiding his expression. "Smoke, movement. On the ground, signs that people have been through. We help people as much as protect the town. You've been the first in almost two years. In the beginning, there were more."

"Not all good?"

"Of course not. We turned some bad people away. They didn't seem tempted to come back, but the town wasn't anywhere near what it is now."

"Where did you come from?" It was out of my mouth before I thought twice about it.

"I grew up just outside of Horsham. My parents had a bit of land where they kept horses. My Dad was away a lot because of the army. He'd go off on tour to Iraq, Timor, Afghanistan. So, it was just me and my Mum a lot of the time. I joined up after I finished school. It was like the family business, you know? My grandfather was a digger and my Dad was, so it was only natural."

He didn't seem to want to stop talking, so I just let him go. "My Dad retired from active duty right before I went to Afghanistan. He did it to be closer to my Mum, who was already terminal. He went around to high schools doing these talks about how noble a career in the defense force was. I bet he didn't tell them the part about shooting people. You'd think they'd get it, right? Nothing prepares you for killing someone. Nothing."

I took my gaze off the horizon. It was quiet out there, nothing moved except the rustling of the wind. I forced myself to look at Shaw, who had hunched forward, arms crossed over his knees. He'd said his Mum was terminal. That almost always meant cancer.

"I was over there almost six months before I got a call from Dad saying that Mum's cancer had come back. He said her headaches had been getting worse and she'd started seeing things. The doctors put her on chemo and heavy medication to shrink the tumor in her brain, but it wasn't enough. They couldn't even operate. She died before I could come back. I'll regret it for the rest of my life, not being there. But, at least I remember her when she was well."

"I bet she was proud of you." It seemed the right thing to say.

"I guess."

We fell silent then and it seemed neither of us knew what to say next. I sat there awkwardly, scanning the horizon, overly aware of him next to me.

"I've got verbal diarrhea today, sorry," he shrugged, trying to make a joke.

I offered him a half-hearted smile, trying to avoid his eyes.

"What were your parents like?" he asked suddenly and my eyebrows shot up in surprise. I thought I'd made it clear that I didn't like questions.

"They were good people," I said.

"Were they…" he began, but stopped, wringing his hands nervously.

The day I'd left was the last time I'd spoken to my parents.

It was a miracle the phones were still working and later on I realized it was how they found me. The Quarantine Officers. They'd traced the lines to root out anyone who was hiding. Luckily for me, I'd left ten seconds before they bashed down my front door.

I looked at the land-line, wondering if it still worked. I picked up the receiver and when I heard a dial tone I wondered if I should take the risk and call Mum and Dad. If I was going to get out of here, I'd take them. Of course I would. So, I dialed the number that had never changed and it rang.

I had no friends. I'd forgotten how to relate to people I'd been so hell bent on not getting hurt again. I had my parents and Jase and Meg. I knew the guys at the gym, I beat their asses every other day, but they weren't my friends. There was no one else I wanted to save. No one else I wanted to call.

"Hello?" It was my Mum. She sounded afraid.

"Mum? It's Prue."

"Prue?"

"Yes Mum, I'm coming to get you and Dad. Okay? I'm coming over and we can get out of here."

"No! Prue, stay away."

"Mum?"

"We're sick, sweetie. Your father and I are sick." I could tell she was trying not to cry.

"No," I gasped, already feeling tears welling. They couldn't be sick. They couldn't be.

"Prue, you have to get out. It's too late for us. You have to go."

"Mum?"

Then Dad was on the phone. "Listen, Prudence." I knew he meant business when he used my full name. "The town's going into Quarantine. The only chance you have is if you get out. You have to go now. Don't speak to anyone, don't touch anyone. Take what you can and go bush and stay there. Find shelter and running water."

"Dad." Tears were running down my face. "What about Jase?"

"I told him the same thing."

"Okay."

"Prue, we love you, honey. Always remember that we love you. Have faith. Keep going. Things will get better, you'll see."

"I love you, Dad." I could hear Mum crying in the background. I was on speaker. "I love you, Mum. Always."

"Go." That was the last thing I ever heard my Dad say.

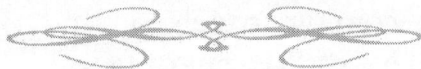

* * *

Shaw was looking at me with something like pity in his eyes.

I scowled, looking away and snapped, "Everyone has a pity story. Whatever."

"Doesn't make it hurt any less."

"It doesn't matter."

"Of course it does."

He *was* one of the good ones. He was nice and understanding and all of those things that people tell you you should be. He was all of those things without even trying. And it pissed me off.

"You find me infuriating," he said suddenly.

Infuriatingly attractive. Everyone had a little bit of a dickhead in them. Where the hell was his? "You should be watching the horizon," I said, ignoring him.

"There's nothing out here, Prue. At least not in a two kilometer radius." He knew I was trying to push him away.

"Then we should get down."

"Prue." He made to take my hand and I jerked away. I wanted him to touch me so much.

"Don't." It would start out nice, but inevitably it would come to an end and where did I have to go but out here again.

"I just want to help you," he said, the hurt plain in his voice.

"You're all so worried about helping me. Just help yourself. I'm fine."

"You can't do everything alone, Prue. You don't have to anymore."

I sighed, standing. "Before. After. It's all the same."

"What's that supposed to mean?"

I began to climb down from the roof the way we'd come up and tried to keep my temper in check. Just leave me alone, Shaw. It's better that way. But, he was after me so fast I didn't have a chance. He grasped my arm, sending bolts of electricity or whatever it was meant to be, up and down my skin.

"I didn't mean to piss you off," he said thinly.

I shrugged.

"Stop shrugging, Prue. It doesn't suit you."

"Then what does?"

He narrowed his eyes, letting out a long breath through his nose. I didn't like the look of his face one bit. Luckily for him, he didn't reply and let me go. "I don't camp here," he said, his voice clipped. "I know a good place not far, but still a few hours walk."

"Fine." Walking was fine. It was the talking I didn't like.

Shaw's campsite was a small ditch at the base of some trees. It was a smart choice, really. It offered shelter from the wind and cut us off from view of anyone who might be around. The trees would diffuse any light from a campfire, so all in all, it was a perfect place to spend the night.

Dinner consisted of some dried fruit and meal bars that someone had made up back at the town and some of Nan's hard bread and cheese. Didn't sound like much, but it was much better than I was used to. Shat all over the gritty damper I'd cooked in the ground in the middle of summer.

"I'll take first watch," Shaw said as he fiddled with the fire, and I wondered if he'd let go of our little argument earlier. "We'll halve it if you want."

"Okay."

"I'll wake you about two am. I usually leave around six."

I nodded, the talking already exhausting and settled into the blankets, my head against the end of my pack. I'd slept like this so many times it was familiar and I drifted off quickly. Back in town, sleeping in a bed was weird and I could never manage to drift off completely. Strange how you become used to things.

It could have been that disoriented moment right before you wake up, but I swore I felt fingertips brush my cheek. Stirring, I realized Shaw's hand was on my shoulder coaxing me awake and my eyes flew open.

"Time to swap," he whispered in the semi-darkness. He'd let the fire die down to embers and it cast little light over the clearing.

"What time is it?"

"Almost three thirty."

"You were meant to wake me at two," I said, annoyed. I knew why he did it, but he shouldn't have bothered. He didn't need to take care of me. I could do that myself.

He shrugged and we swapped places and this time, his head was where mine had been. I didn't stop to think about *that*. He was asleep as fast as I had been and I sat near the fire, listening to the bush. Nothing stirred, except for the chirping of a lone cicada somewhere out in the darkness.

For a moment, I cast my eyes over Shaw's sleeping form, taking in the sharp lines of his face. Why the hell did he have to be so handsome? And why did he seem so interested in me? Sometimes I thought it was because I was new. Other times I got the feeling it was more than that. I was drawn to him like a magnet and I didn't know how to take it. I'd never felt like that around anyone before.

Shaking my head, I turned my back to him and looked at my watch. Four. Two hours till sun-up and two hours alone with my thoughts. And for the first time in three years of putting up with myself, I didn't want them.

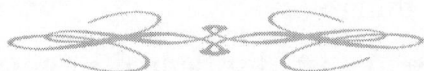

It was around lunch time the next day when Shaw led me to a line of windbreaker trees at one edge of an open paddock. In the corner was a small dam, full of water, low in the ground and protected from line of sight in three-sixty degrees.

He dumped his pack in the ground and stretched his back. "Up for a swim?"

I raised my eyebrows at him, glancing at the dam. Somehow I didn't think this was part of Captain Wallis' game plan.

"I come here all the time. It's safe."

Like that was reassuring.

"Suit yourself," he laughed and to my utter embarrassment, he pulled off his trademark kaki shirt, kicked off his boots and socks and stripped down to his boxers. Wading into the muddy water he looked back over his shoulder with a grin. "What?"

"Nothing." I tried not to look at his naked chest, but that's all there was. The end of the world had given him a toned physique, but he probably was that way before, being in the Army.

"Are you coming in?"

I looked around the paddock, but we were alone. Of course we were. Shaw wasn't stupid enough to horse around when there could have been danger about.

"Have you forgotten how to have fun?" he asked darkly, when I still didn't move.

Feeling bold, I scowled, pulling off my shirt and Shaw's eyes nearly fell out of his head. Suddenly, I was glad Hannah had given me that black lace bra at the shop. I bet he thought I'd go swimming fully clothed.

I wasn't the best swimmer. I'd done laps occasionally at the gym, but I never put my head underwater. The thought of it running up my nose and drowning me was a bit too much to handle. That, and chlorine burned. This water was pure rain, tinted a beige brown from the clay earth of the dam, but not dirty in the least. The only thing that might be in it was a lost eel or a leech or two.

Ignoring Shaw's eyes on me, I pulled off my boots and dropped my shorts on top of the pile and stepped gingerly into the shallow end, the cool water soothing my hot feet.

This was one layer away from skinny dipping and that was something I'd never done. I wasn't that kind of girl, but here I was in my underwear with a handsome, ripped man who'd saved my life. Who wouldn't be turned on?

When I hit the deep end the water was only up to my armpits and I looked up at Shaw, who was still staring at me with his weird green eyes and my heart thudded against the inside of my chest. My mind instantly went to that dirty place where my hands ran over his chest and he kissed me and I could almost feel his weight on top of me. I blinked hard. To break the spell and cool myself off before he caught on, I ducked underneath the surface for a moment, the darkness and the flow of water calming. But, when I came back up for air, he was still staring.

"What?" I asked, water dripping down my face. He was so annoying.

"You're beautiful," he blurted and instantly turned red.

"Better rub your eyes, you've got shit in them."

"No," he said carefully. "I meant it."

I shrugged, turning away. Bending my knees so I was immersed up to my neck, I moved my hands back and forth, feeling the pull of water through my fingers. That, and I was kind of embarrassed that I was almost naked after he'd said *that*.

"Do you like coming out to the waste?" I asked as he settled beside me.

He frowned for a moment, then said, "I prefer the quiet. I always did."

"Why?"

"I grew up in the bush," he shrugged, sending out a ripple of water. "I never got on well in the city. Out here it's calm. You can think."

I had been the opposite. I'd lived in London. In Melbourne. Huge cities. I'd been a commuter on the road to whatever it was I was on the road to. "I liked the city," I said. "There was always something to do."

"Yeah, I guess. But nothing is ever simple."

"No, it wasn't."

"You can't see the stars in the city."

My head snapped up at his words and an image flashed in my mind of the first few nights after Quarantine. Lying in a hiding place in the bush, looking up at the sky and feeling so alone and insignificant, hoping to god that I would get some sleep and actually wake up the next morning.

"What is it?" Shaw asked, and I realized I must have some weird expression on my face.

"I used to look up at the sky and wonder what was going to happen. After, you know." It was out my mouth before I realized and I looked away before he could see it had worked me up.

"There's billions of stars up there," Shaw said, and I knew he was trying to cover up the fact that he'd drawn something out of me. "We can't see all of them. Someone told me once that it takes so long for their light to reach Earth, that we're looking into the past. The sky is like a time machine."

"Really? Who said that?"

"My Mum," he said. "She was into stargazing."

"Oh."

Neither of us seemed to know what to say then. It was so easy to talk about the crap things, because that's all that seemed to happen. What else was there to discuss?

"You talk a lot more out here," Shaw said, a curious look on his face.

I grimaced. "I guess there's less people." I never did well with public speaking.

"Why do you call the bush, the waste?"

"It's the wasteland of human existence."

Shaw let out a laugh. "Well, this has got depressing." He sunk back into the water and splashed me.

Blinking in surprise I cried, "Hey."

"What you gunna do about it?" he grinned.

I swept my hands over the surface and sent a huge torrent of water over him.

"Oh, I see how it is," he cried, and splashed me back just as hard.

We went back and forth a few times, and I felt my face split into a grin. He was right. I had forgotten how to have fun. When he didn't splash me back after a while, I stood there, forgetting that my almost naked chest was on display and caught him looking at me weirdly again.

"Why are you looking at me like that?" I asked, frowning.

"I haven't seen you smile before. Not like that."

He stood so close, I could almost feel him and despite everything, he was breaking through. He was invading that place inside of me I thought was dead and lost forever. Underneath the water, I felt his hand brush against my arm, then it was hard against my skin, his thumb running up and down. Looking up, I couldn't understand the look on his face. The one that said, *I want you.* I mean, I understood the intention, I just didn't understand *why*.

All this time, I didn't believe that he was serious. I thought he was just being nice because of what I'd been through. Now, I understood it was more to him. He wanted more.

My breath started to come quickly as he moved closer, the water ripping out around us. Did I want to kiss him? My entire body said yes, but my head said hell no. Shaw had no idea who I was. The kind of person I had to become to survive. The kind of person I still struggled with. A monster lived inside of me and I didn't want him to see it. If he did, then he would see me for what I truly was and he wouldn't want me. He wouldn't even want to look at me. I couldn't deal with that kind of hurt. Not now.

Before this half-naked swim could get any worse, I pulled away a little too sharply and waded back out of the dam.

"Prue?" he called after me as I began pulling my clothes back on.

"This was stupid," I said quietly, knowing full well that the silence would carry the sound straight back to him.

Water splashed behind me, signaling Shaw's exit from the dam.

"We need to get moving," I continued. "We won't make your next marker."

"Yeah, we will," he breathed behind me.

I didn't turn around, lacing my boots back on. "I'd feel better about it if we went."

He seemed to get that he'd pushed me too far and pulled on his own clothes over his wet boxers.

Shouldering my pack, I waited for him and he took the lead, moving through the line of trees. I watched his back in front of me a little in disappointment and a little in relief. That had gotten so close to being something else, it scared the hell out of me. After all that time alone, coming back into some sense of civilization was hard to handle. I'd been telling myself that Shaw would break my heart, when in reality it was the other way around. He would see me and I would break him.

I'd been broken by so many other people I couldn't do that to him. I knew what it was like. And in this world, it would be a billion times worse. He had to stay away from me. I had to forget about the way he made me feel. No good would come of it.

When we got to Shaw's next marker, it was almost dark. I'd been right, but I didn't say anything. The rest of the walk had been uneventful. No movement, no animals. Nothing.

We stopped in a line of gum trees, a small clearing in the center large enough for us to camp the night. I left Shaw to set up a small fire, while I walked the perimeter, checking for tracks, but it was useless in this murky half-light. I'd dropped my pack, but I still had my sword flung over my back. I never felt right without it.

The sound of a branch snapping, drew my attention back to the clearing and my eyes scanned the darkness. It didn't sound like it came from the camp, but things had a weird way of echoing in the bush. Regardless, I made my way back towards Shaw silently, keeping to the darkest parts of the tree line. I'd learnt the hard way that nothing was as it seemed out here. Other people wandered alone and if I could do it for this long, so could they.

I could make out Shaw through the trees, right were I'd left him, but my heart flew to my throat when I saw movement behind him. A man edged out of the cover of the gums and I instantly knew I had to get behind him. Right now, Shaw was smack bang in the middle and had no idea how much shit he was in. His pack was on the ground and the rifle was there with it. He was defenseless.

I hadn't been made yet, so I moved through the trees, circling around, placing my feet carefully on the packed earth, avoiding any leaf litter and bark on the ground. I was almost there when the man raised his arm and moonlight glinted off metal. He had a gun. His presence was made when he clicked the safety off and Shaw turned, coming face to face with the barrel.

"Shit," he hissed.

"On your knees," the man hissed, shoving the gun barrel hard into his chest.

Shaw must have known that he had no choice because he dropped to his knees, shoulders tense.

I was directly behind the man now and stepped forward a few paces, my footfalls silent. I couldn't be sure if Shaw had seen me in the murky light, but if I signaled him I would give myself away.

The closer I came, the more I noticed how thin the would-be thief was. Bones were protruding through the skin of his arms and even his hair looked stringy and sparse. This was a desperate man. He stood right in front of Shaw and aimed the gun execution style. The rest seemed to happen in slow motion.

The man didn't see me come up behind as he silently debated whether he was going to pull the trigger. He was too fixated on Shaw to notice. When he clicked the safety on and off again, I knew I had to make a choice and it was a no-brainer. I chose Shaw. Without hesitation, I stepped lightly to the side with my left foot, the sword arcing cleanly through the air. The man didn't know what hit him as I severed his forearm, the gun clattering to the ground. Without interrupting the flow of the blade, I pivoted on my right foot and brought the sword down into the man's throat. I didn't break stance as the man crumbled to the ground, dead.

There was nothing but silence for a minute before I lowered the sword and looked back at Shaw, who was white as a ghost and breathing hard. Blood had splattered across his cheek. Surely, he'd seen someone die before? He'd been in a war zone. Surely?

"Are you okay?" I asked, when he didn't say anything.

"Yeah." He grabbed the hem of his shirt and wiped the blood off his face. I couldn't help but notice that his hands were shaking.

I crouched by the man and wiped the sword clean on his tattered shirt before sheathing it. Out of habit, I went through his pockets, relieving him of a knife and a few bullets. I picked up the gun, which looked like a poorly cared for revolver of some kind, clicked the safety back on and put it in my pack.

"How the hell did you do that?" Shaw was watching me steal off a corpse. What the hell did I look like?

I shrugged. "Like you said, it's been three years. I've adapted."

"But," he began, but I cut him off.

"We need to get away from here. Now."

Shaw understood and picked up his discarded pack as I donned mine.

"He came from the south east. Before, I was moving north away from people in the south. He may have come from there." It was the most I had said in one breath in years. If Shaw noticed, he didn't say anything.

I almost had to drag him through the bush. He'd withdrawn into himself and seemed to be in some kind of shock. I knew his Dad had been shot after the virus. He'd told me as much and I wondered if it had anything to do with his reaction. Now wasn't the time to talk it out.

We walked as far as we dared in the darkness. The moon was only a quarter full and it cast very little light over the countryside. Eventually we stopped, taking cover in a little copse of trees. The space around us was so open it felt ominous, pressing down on my shoulders. I doubted that I'd get any rest tonight.

The feeling of dread that had built in my heart at the dam earlier surfaced as the threat of discovery lessened, and I felt sick. This was exactly the thing I didn't want Shaw to witness. He'd seen what I was capable of now and something like that couldn't be unseen. I wouldn't change it, the alternative was his brains splattered on the ground, but now... my heart felt empty because I think he'd just vacated it. I didn't want to start anything, but I don't think I had a choice. It was doing it of it's own free will.

He would be naive to assume that I hadn't done this before. Kill a man. Hell, I'd just saved his life.

I guess now we were even.

Ten

I made Shaw walk through the darkness, none of the places we came across satisfied my scrutiny. It was safer to keep moving, even in the dark. Experience taught me distance from people was the best option, despite the risk of a broken ankle.

He followed behind me, hardly making a sound and I hoped he was switched on enough to follow my footsteps. Truthfully, I was worried about him. It was one thing to be deployed to Afghanistan and another to see a girl half your size slice through a desperate man with a sword. I'd have to talk to him about it, even though it would pain me to do so. I didn't want to hear what he thought of me. I couldn't handle knowing… It wouldn't be real until he actually said the words.

Prudence Ashford is a monster.

A branch snapped somewhere out in the darkness and I halted, Shaw behind me. Had we been followed? I was sure we were alone. Maybe it was just an animal. Please be an animal.

Abruptly, my head snapped to the side as I heard a keening sound coming from the darkness. I hadn't heard that noise in a long time. They sounded like whale songs, clicking and whistling. I had never thought the human voice was capable of such a thing, but a lot of things had been turned on their head.

When I had been desperate enough to venture close to a town to scavenge, I would hear them call to each other in the night. In the beginning, I would hide myself in small hard to reach places and hope to hell that they wouldn't find me. Even out in the waste, away from the remains of civilization, but they'd never wandered.

"Prue?" Shaw whispered, when he caught my sudden movement.

There was a low whining sound again off in the darkness and I covered Shaw's mouth with a hand and pulled him down. His eyes widened with surprise, but he didn't say anything. I touched a finger to my ear and pointed to our right. A low whistle and click echoed across the open paddock ahead. I knew he heard it this time.

I felt Shaw tense beside me and I placed a finger to my lips. Be quiet.

The fact that one of those things was out here didn't bode well. There was a hell of a lot of nothing for k's. Only the odd farm or roadside pub to break up the dreary countryside. We were lucky it was only the one. It was out there somewhere, prowling the darkness, looking for something to eat and I'd rather it not be us.

I lifted my right hand and rested it on the hilt of my sword, gently tugging it loose, ready to draw if it came our way. I wasn't sure how they hunted, but smell must have something to do with it. If it caught our scent, then we would have to kill it.

There was a high pitched squeal that was abruptly cut off with a snap, the sound echoing from across the open paddock. I took the opportunity to drag Shaw backwards and we ran as silently as we could, getting as much distance between us as possible while it ate. South-west, away from it and the clearing and back towards the town, albeit going south, but still in the vicinity.

I fisted my hand into Shaw's shirt and dragged him along behind me. How much shit could we get into in one night? Nothing for ages and now this? What the hell did we do to deserve this? Nothing, but that's just how it was.

When I was finally satisfied we were far enough away, I dumped my pack on the ground near a little patch of bushes. Open paddock, slight cover. If we didn't light a fire, we'd be camouflaged until morning. Looking at the watch Shaw had given me, it said it was three am.

"Get some sleep," I whispered and Shaw jumped, his eyes wide. "I'll keep watch till morning."

He didn't argue or complain. He didn't say anything. Pulling out his blanket, he just curled up on the ground and went to sleep. Just like that. Pulling out my own blanket, I put it over him with a sigh and stood vigil for the rest of the night, eyes and ears open for trouble.

Dawn came without incident.

I don't know if it was morbid curiosity or just that I wanted visual confirmation, but we walked back to the paddock without discussing it. Shaw wanted to know as much as I did.

I stared down at what remained of the kangaroo and grimaced. The fact that it was mutilated was proof enough for me. I imagined the man who'd attacked us was in much the same state. If they could follow their prey by scent, then the blood would have drawn it. I didn't know for sure though, the wind had been flat last night.

"Do you know what it was?" It was the first thing Shaw had said since the night before.

"It was one of them."

"One of who?" Hadn't he come across one before? He spent a lot of time out here, why was he even asking?

I gave him a look. "Are there any buildings near by?"

"There's a pub and servo down the road about a kilometer that way," he pointed roughly east. "Other than that, there's nothing for ages."

"I want to go there." I wanted to go find it and kill it before it found us or the town.

"What? Why?"

"They don't like the sun," I shrugged.

"You want to go after the thing that did that?" He pointed at the remains of the kangaroo. He didn't seem to like the idea very much.

"It will hunt us next."

"Prue..."

I didn't want to discuss it, so I just walked off in the direction he'd pointed. He could follow if he wanted or he could just go home.

"Wait," he called after me.

I stopped abruptly and waited, not bothering to turn around. Then he was beside me and I didn't have the guts to look him in the face. There was a wall between us now and there was no fixing it.

"I'll show you the way," he said and moved off, dry grass crunching under his boots.

And so started our next silent walk into who knows what. I clamped down my wandering thoughts and focused on the task at hand. Dwelling would be counter-productive and this was no game we were playing.

When the pub came into view, my stomach dropped. When we stood on the side of the cracked, two lane highway that passed out the front, I swallowed hard. It was an old brick building with a tin verandah and ivy had taken over the facade, cracking it in several places. The signage was still intact, advertising beer on tap and that there was meals seven days a week in the bistro. From the looks of the place the bistro was just the bar. It didn't look that big.

"What's the plan?" Shaw's voice brought me back to life.

"I'll kill it."

"I'm going with you." He stepped forward, pulling the rifle off his shoulder.

I pushed him back and loosened my sword. "No."

"Prue…"

"Don't worry about me," I said pointedly and he grimaced, taking a step back. "Keep watch."

Giving him one last look, I drew my sword and pushed against the door to the front bar, easing it open. It swung inwards silently and I stepped inside, conscious of Shaw's eyes on my back. I hadn't exactly sought one of these things out before, but how hard could it be? Look for the darkest place and stick it with the pointy end.

The pub was small inside and they seemed to have small brains, so there wasn't many places it could hide if it was here. The front room consisted of a long bar and a room full of tables. The end closest to me had an old pool table that was covered with a thick layer of dust and grit and to my left was a door through to the kitchen. But, I didn't have to go very far to find what I was looking for.

It was standing in the far corner, wreathed in shadows, its back to the room. Sunlight streamed through the windows between me and it, but if it got a whiff of me, it wouldn't stop it for long.

It had been months and months since I'd had an encounter and despite myself, I looked it over. There was no way of telling who it once was. Its clothing was torn and covered in dirt and dry brown blood, like it was slowly rotting away. If it wasn't for the slight rise and fall of its shoulders, I would have sworn it was dead. That, and it was standing upright.

Looking over the floor, it was relatively free of debris. The windows had been smashed in at some point and glass and wood was scattered, but towards the far side where the bar was, there was a clear path straight to the corner. I had to kill it before it knew I was there. I had no idea if I could take it on otherwise. I'd seen them in full flight and they were fast when confronted with food. And I was food.

The last thing I would want was Shaw mopping up after

me, or worse, come in here and be torn apart too. No, this had to end my way.

Placing one foot in front of the other, I moved across the partially lit room inch by inch, my footfalls soft against the hardwood floor. My eye flickered up to the corner for a second and that's when I stood on a pace of glass and it cracked loudly in the silence. Abruptly, I halted, my heart thumping painfully in my chest. When it didn't move, I let out a slow breath.

A full minute passed before I began my advance again.

How would I do it? What would kill it the quickest? Chop it's head off. The sword was sharp enough, that would have to do.

Raising the blade, I leveled it with the mutant's neck and pulled back, ready to swing. Before I could finish it off, it's head snapped back and it let out a piercing screech, turning to face me. My eyes widened in fear as it fixed on me and I swung, the blade arcing through the air and cutting through emancipated, leathery flesh.

Abruptly, it's screeching was cut off as it's head fell to the floor with a thud, it's limp body following. I let out a sigh of relief, my shoulders sagging forward, the tip of the sword against the floor. There was a bang behind me as the outer door opened and I swung around, automatically pointing the sword out in front to defend myself.

My heart stuck in my throat as my eyes collided with Shaw's. He stood just inside the door, rifle aimed right at me and this seemed so familiar it made me ache. We stood there for a moment in complete silence, until I lowered the sword, tearing my eyes away.

"Are you okay?" he asked.

No. "Yes."

He crossed the room, eyes flickering to the kitchen, but nothing else had attacked, so it was fair to assume that it had been the only one hiding in here. We'd only heard one last night. I was positive of it.

Shaw stood beside me, taking in the remains of the mutant like he'd never seen anything like it in his entire life. "What the fuck is it?"

I frowned at him, confused. "You've never seen them?"

"No, I think I would remember."

"The sick." It was all I had to say.

"Prue, the sick were burnt. Their bodies were burnt." He had a horrified look on his face.

Who was there to burn the last of them? It could have been worse. It could have been another kind of plague. The kind you saw in TV shows or movies. But it wasn't. We should feel lucky that there was only a few.

I shook my head. There was always one who got out, wasn't there? Just like in a horror movie, there's always one last scene. Just when you think you're safe, the serial killer comes out from underneath the bed and slashes the hero. You feel bad for them, you want a happy ending. But that's just not how life works.

"When you talked about them, I always thought you meant other people. This was who you meant, wasn't it."

I nodded.

"Why haven't I come across any?"

He seemed to be asking himself, but I answered anyway. "There aren't many. Not here. The city, maybe more."

"In other words, don't go to Melbourne."

"No."

"What are they? Zombies?"

I snorted. Zombies? This wasn't the movies. "Mutants."

"The virus mutated the survivors instead of killing them?"

"I guess." Did I look like a scientist?

"And they're hungry," he said disgusted, obviously remembering the remains of the kangaroo.

"What would you do if you were desperate for food?" I asked, cocking my head to the side.

"Point."

"We need to go back." It wasn't a question. "If it's out here, then one could find the town."

Shaw nodded, his eyes running over the mutant again and I reached behind the bar for a rag, cleaning the strange red blood off my sword. It was thick, like jam. Congealed. I didn't want to know what that meant.

Outside, the day was full and bright. Nothing had stirred after the horrible noise the mutant had made and we were safe to move into the bush, avoiding the road and crossing into farmland. Luckily the path I'd chosen was back towards the town and we didn't have to pass near the place where Shaw was attacked.

After that, it would have been the cherry on the cake to lay eyes on whatever was left of his attacker. And now that Shaw seemed to be talking to me again, even if it was short, I didn't want to see it either.

It took us the best part of the day to get back to the town and the sun was low when the wall came into sight. In a way, I was glad to be back, to have a respite from the carnage of the last twenty-four hours, but there was still the underlying fear I'd squashed inside. Now that he had time to think about it, what would Shaw do? What would he say to Captain about what I did? What would they do, now that they knew what I was capable of?

Deep down, I didn't want to lose Shaw, but I knew I already had. The last thing I had to lose was my home. That's what this town had somehow become and I wasn't sure if I belonged here anymore and if I ever did.

"Hey!" A voice called out from on top of the wall.

Shaw raised his hand. "It's Shaw and Prue."

"Open the gate," came the voice again and I realized it was Bobby.

The squeal of corrugated iron pierced the silence as the gate was eased open and we slid through into safety. Bobby came down the ladder to meet us, his shotgun slung over his back.

"You're back way too early," he said concerned as he stopped in front of us. "Are you guys okay?"

Shaw shook his head. "We need to speak to Captain, right away."

Eleven

I sat awkwardly across from Captain Wallis in his kitchen, overly aware of Shaw next to me. He hadn't once looked at me since we walked through the gate. My eyes settled on my pack and sword by the fridge and I couldn't help envisioning everything I'd done with it in the past twenty-four hours.

Luckily, I didn't have to say anything because Shaw was giving a report like he was still in the army. A short, clinical account of our run-in with the mutant. "Prue said they were the sick." I couldn't help but notice his voice faltered when he said my name.

"What do you mean?" Captain asked, turning to me for the first time since we'd sat down.

"The sick that got better." I couldn't put it more simply than that.

"We came across one in the night," Shaw continued. "It was hunting out in the middle of nowhere. We got away without it noticing, but when we went back in the morning all that was left was a mutilated kangaroo."

"Bloody hell," Captain cursed.

"Prue hunted the mutant down and took care of it."

Captain looked at me with a strange expression. Was he sizing me up? Did he think I wasn't capable of defending myself? "How did you find out about them?"

"A few months after," I started, "I went home."

"God." Captain ran a hand over his face.

I didn't know how to explain the terror I'd felt hiding in that kitchen cupboard all the time ago, so I just said, "I didn't go back."

"And you say they only stick to the towns?"

"Yes."

"Why would one have been out in the middle of nowhere? If they don't like the sun, then that's a mark of desperation."

"They must be running out of food," Shaw said quietly.

"So, that's why you think they're wandering the countryside?" Captain asked.

I nodded. That was exactly it.

"I wonder," he continued. "If they're running out of food and abandoning the towns, have they tried to eat each other?"

"It would certainly eliminate most of the threat if they did," Shaw said, not looking at me.

"If they got a whiff of the cattle, then they'd be done for," Captain mused. "Thanks, Prue. We'll be able to put some defensive measures in place before things get dire."

I smiled thinly, my heart not in it.

"Keep this under wraps until we can think over this," Captain said. "We don't want to go causing a panic. If we need to disclose this, it'll be done properly. The last thing we need is wild rumors being flung over town."

"Of course not," Shaw said.

I nodded my understanding.

"If that's all, you two better go get cleaned up and have a rest. I appreciate you coming back so directly and giving me the information. I'm sure Mayor Thompson would say the same once I've read him in."

"Thank you, sir," Shaw said, sliding his chair back from the table. Wasn't he going to say anything about the man who tried to kill him? I looked up at him, my eyes wide, but he didn't acknowledge me. I wasn't about to oust him, so I got up and shouldered my pack, iweight of my sword on my hand.

Outside, it was already twilight and stars were beginning to shine through the deepening sky. Shaw hesitated out on the footpath and I stopped next to him wondering if I should just walk off and let it be.

"You should go see if Nan needs anything," he said, not looking me in the eye.

I didn't know what to stay to make it better, so I decided to leave it alone. Without a word, I turned and walked down the darkening street, my shoulder aching from my heavy pack. He didn't call out after me and I sighed, kicking a loose stone across the asphalt.

I knew this was going to happen, so why did it hurt so much? I had to switch it off. I knew I could do it because it was the thing that got me through the past three years alive. But now, maybe it was my biggest problem.

When I opened the front door to Nan's I saw a warm glow coming from the lounge room. I called out as I came in, so I wouldn't startle her.

"Prue?" came her voice. "Is that you?"

I dumped my bag in the hallway and tiptoed into the lounge as I was want to do and she stood sharply when she saw my face.

"Are you okay, dear?" Nan asked, opening her arms.

I didn't know if I should burden her with the awful truth. She would say something nice and I probably didn't deserve it. Shaw probably didn't want me to mention his near death experience and Captain had told us to keep quiet about the mutant. Maybe Shaw was embarrassed that I'd saved him. I didn't know what to think. My thoughts were all mixed up.

I let her embrace me and I said, "I'm pretty tired, I guess." I hadn't slept in over a day. I was beat.

Nan frowned, looking me over. "Are you hungry? I have a little left over from tea if you are. Then you better run off to bed."

She sat me down in the kitchen and pulled out a container from the esky she kept on the kitchen counter. None of the houses had gas or electricity anymore, so there was a solar powered storm lamp set on the middle of the table, casting it's cold light over everything. Soon a bowl of vegetable soup was put in front of me with a chunk of bread and butter. Nan really took good care of me and right now I was so grateful for it, even though I could never tell her what had happened. She still cared for me. At least someone did.

I think I slept almost twelve hours all told. By the time I finally woke, it was about eleven in the morning. Captain said not to worry about reporting to the wall today, but I had nothing else to do. So after washing up, I went and volunteered to keep my mind occupied.

Captain set me on the wall as an extra patrol. It was my job to walk the perimeter and watch the spaces we didn't have the coverage on. And in the event something did happen, I'd be used as a runner. I didn't mind walking the wall. I mean, it was better than sitting in one spot and when I sat still, my mind wandered all kinds of places these days.

To my surprise, Shaw had the exact same thought. As I passed a ladder, he was climbing up, rifle slung across his back and my heart twisted. He hadn't seen me, so I went on, not sure if I should linger. I'd see him on the way around and maybe by then I'd work up the courage to say something.

I hadn't had an opportunity to ask him if he was okay, what with all the monster hunting. That was the icing *and* the cherry on top. When I inevitably came round to his position, he didn't hear me approach, my footfalls light on the wooden platform.

"Are you alright?" I asked in my quiet voice.

He jumped, as if his mind had been elsewhere. "Yeah," he said. "It was a long one, you know."

I knew he was lying, but I didn't want to push my luck.

"What?" he asked, when I just stood there frowning at him.

Casting my eyes downward, I walked around him and continued down the platform. Why ask him when I already knew the answer.

Before I had to pass him again, I climbed down the ladder near the main gate back to ground level for a breather. I needed to collect my thoughts before I had to deal with that again.

I went into the small cottage that had been turned into a guard house. A place where we could dump our stuff, refill water, have something to eat. A place for some time-out. Before, you'd describe it as a staff room. A long porch stretched across the front and a few steps led down to a garden that had once been filled with roses and other flowers, but now it was overgrown, but someone at least seemed to have weeded it.

Perching on the edge of the table, I filled my water bottle from the plastic cask on bench and took a few mouthfuls. I was alone and it felt safe. Alone was safe.

There were footsteps outside on the porch and a heavy sigh as someone sat down. Looking at my feet, I was glad that whoever it was didn't come inside. Putting on a face was right at the bottom of the list of things I wanted to do. Truthfully, my head was filled with Shaw. I knew this was how things were going to be between us now, but I couldn't seem to get over it. Maybe in time, I'd get used to the fact that I had started to soften towards him, then life had pulled a fast one on me. I wasn't meant to be happy. I was meant to be okay for now.

"Hey, Shaw." It was Eva, which meant it was Shaw who was sitting out on the porch. My heart skipped a beat and I suddenly hated myself.

This was going to be painful. Whatever Eva had to say to him would be either one of two things. One; how she wanted to marry him and have his babies. Or two; what was wrong with him, which meant a long conversation about me and my barbaric ways. Shaw didn't have it in him to tell her about what happened out there... did he? He was a good guy, he wouldn't...

"Are you okay?" Eva's voice grated on my nerves more than usual.

"Yeah." How he meant to fool her was beyond me when that word came out sounding so defeated.

"*Shaw.*"

"Eva, I..."

"You can tell me if something's bothering you."

"Sure."

"Did something happen out there?"

"A lot of things happen out there."

"Shaw. I can handle it you know. I might be a sweet school teacher, but I understand what the world has changed into."

There was silence for what seemed like forever and I still couldn't move. "If it wasn't for Prue..."

"What did she do?" Eva sounded horrified and my jaw tightened.

"She saved me. But, it was how she did it. She just cut him down without batting an eyelid." And there it was. The thing I didn't want to hear. I felt a tear sliding down my face and I brushed it away, annoyed with myself.

"She killed a man?"

"To save me."

"Of course, Shaw. Of course she did, but it's bothering you…"

"She didn't seem to care. I mean, it seemed easy. Just to stand there and do it."

Of course I fucking cared, I wanted to scream. I didn't want to hurt anyone. I never wanted to hurt anyone. But they wanted to hurt me. Was I supposed to let them kill and rape me? Was I meant to lay down and die?

"She was out there alone."

"I know, Eva."

"It would have changed anyone."

His answering sigh was so sharp, I heard it inside. Why was he telling her any of this? The few times I'd seen them together he'd seemed exasperated. I could think of one thing that had changed his opinion of me and he'd already said it. The way I had killed that man. The way I had stepped up and felt nothing when blood coated my sword. When it had sliced through his emancipated arm like soft butter. The moment I saved *Shaw* from death.

That's the moment his opinion of me changed. And it hurt more than I thought it would.

"Do you think she could be... I mean…"

"A danger to the town?" Shaw finished off for her, but his tone didn't even register with me. All I heard was the word danger.

I'd been alone for so long. Even before the virus wiped everyone out and changed the world. The moment it began to change for the better, the moment I began to feel something other than emptiness... something happens to take it away. The fact of life is that there are no happy endings. It's just happy for now, because tomorrow it'll all be gone. I'm better off not being happy in the first place. I suddenly felt like crying.

I didn't want to hurt anyone. I didn't want to live like that anymore, but if I had to live with that question over my head for the rest of my life… the one that asked if I was a danger to everyone here, everyone that had shown me kindness… then, maybe I was better off out there.

Taking a deep breath to collect myself, I wondered how I'd get out of the house. If I stood there in the kitchen for much longer, they could come in and see me and then they would know I had been listening. Or someone would come looking and call me out. The only way I could go was directly past them, head down and fast. They would suspect, but they wouldn't know.

I grabbed my water bottle and pushed the screen door open with a violent jab. Not stopping, I thumped down the stairs past Eva and Shaw and strode across the lawn to the ladder. My back burned with the knowledge that they were watching my every move and I felt like throwing up. I'd decided to stay weeks ago, but right now I wanted to run back to that hopeless life out there on my own.

I'd made peace with the person I'd become and now I felt nothing but pain for it.

Twelve

Despite the flaming rejection I felt in my heart, I was determined to show everyone I was well adjusted. Of course I had problems, but I wasn't about to go out and do something to hurt anyone.

I sat on the edge of Hannah's bed, while she poked about in her closet. While Shaw and I were gone, the town decided to plan a party. I remembered he'd said something about having a BBQ back when I was still in his good books. I still thought it was a frivolous idea.

"How about this one?" Hannah asked, holding up a bright blue floral dress.

I made a face and shook my head. She was determined to dress me up like a doll and if it gave the impression I was fine, then I'd let her. Because I was fine. Generally.

"You look enthusiastic about this party."

"Why does there need to be one?" I asked.

"People need to feel hope," she said, rifling through her closet again. "Now more than ever. A party is exactly what we need."

I shrugged, but her back was to me.

"Did something happen out there?" she asked, turning back to me. Worry was plain in her voice.

I shook my head. Captain had asked us not to say anything and I wouldn't.

"You came back early. Everyone is saying something happened."

"Nothing happened." Except Shaw was almost shot and we were almost eaten by mutants. Yeah, nothing happened.

Hannah seemed to accept my explanation. "Was it weird? Being back out there?"

"Yeah."

"Were you sacred? I mean, you don't have to tell me, but after everything… I thought you wouldn't want to go out again."

I shook my head. It was like Stockholm Syndrome. "It's what I know."

Hannah grimaced as if she didn't know what to say, but then she pulled out another dress, abruptly changing the subject and my shoulders sagged in relief. "This is the one," she said, holding up a black number.

Eyeing the dress, I was the one who grimaced this time.

"Try it on. For me." She tore it from the hanger and flung it at me.

She turned her back while I pulled it on and the first thing I thought was that it was way too short, but then again, I was never into wearing dresses. It was my color, though. Black.

"Okay," I said and Hannah turned around and instantly let out a wolf whistle.

"Hot damn," she exclaimed, beaming. "The boys will go nuts."

I looked at my reflection and didn't recognize the woman who looked back. Fashion was low on the priority list and I was sure somewhere along the line I'd forgotten what I looked like. The dress was low cut with spaghetti straps over my shoulders and the hemline just hid the ugly scar on my leg. Maybe it looked alright.

"You're wearing it," Hannah declared, her hands on her hips.

"Fine." I tugged on my socks and combat boots, much to her disgust.

"You're not wearing those?"

"Yes."

"I have some..."

"No, thanks." I gave her a look. If I had to wear this little dress, then I would wear my boots.

Down on the main street, party preparations were in full swing. We'd promised Nan that we'd go down and help out once Hannah was done playing dress ups.

Every so often there were steel drums set up along the road, full of wood and coals and a huge open fire pit that had been rigged with racks and hot plates. I assumed this was the BBQ. Someone had even strung up fairy lights and found some Christmas tinsel. It was very festive and the whole street had changed. It was like the world hadn't died and I wasn't sure what to make of that.

We found Nan outside the shop, setting up a trestle table

with all sort of things. Drinks that consisted of flavored milk for the kids, cordial and some kind of bush iced tea. But, what caught my attention was the pile of baked goods at one end.

"Cupcakes?" I asked, surprised. I'm sure I thought they didn't exist anymore.

"Fairy cakes," Nan proclaimed proudly. "You scoop out the middle in one piece, fill with whipped cream and stick the top back on. Two halves, like that. Looks like wings."

"That's why they're called fairy cakes," Hannah laughed like it was absurd.

"Oh, shoosh. Be grateful you have them," Nan scolded, slapping Hannah's hand away when she reached for one. "Here, Prue. Have one."

I couldn't remember the last time I had cake, so when I bit into it, Nan and Hannah laughed at the expression that flashed across my face. It tasted like... *home.* I almost felt like crying, but someone turned on music and my head flew up.

"Long time, huh?" Hannah asked and I nodded. It had been a long time since things felt this normal. Even though they were still screwed up.

The towns idea of music was a collection of MP3 players and portable speakers that had been rewired to plug into a headphone jack. They seemed to charge them all at the store, where the solar panels were rigged on the roof. They did have quite an impressive selection. Classic rock, country, pop and alternative. If I closed my eyes, I could imagine that nothing had changed.

It wasn't long before the music drew everyone in town and the party was in full swing. The smells of cooking and laughter were everywhere, people were dancing in the middle of the street without a care in the world. Hannah was right. Everyone needed some forgetting.

I hovered around the edges unsure, every so often speaking politely to anyone who came by and said hello, but when I caught Shaw's eye across the street I wasn't quite prepared for the look on his face. He was staring like he'd never seen a girl in a dress before. A dangerous girl in a dress.

When he started walking over, my heart began to beat painfully in my chest and I wondered what he wanted. I couldn't move, even if I wanted to, and I knew I'd have to endure whatever it was he had to say to me.

"Hey," he said quietly, standing in front of me, eyes running over the dress.

I didn't say anything. I didn't know what to say to him anymore. Hey, would have been good start, but even that was beyond me.

"You look nice," he said, biting his bottom lip.

I squirmed. "Thanks. It's Hannah's fault."

He smiled, the first smile he'd given me since that day he dared me to swim in the dam. "Are you enjoying the party?"

"It's not my thing," I said awkwardly.

He let out a slow breath. "Do you want to dance?"

I gave him a look. One minute he was avoiding me, the next he was talking to Eva about my dangerous compulsions behind my back and now he wanted to *dance*?

"C'mon, just one dance," he winked at me. A new song started and he grinned wolfishly. It was a slow one.

I hesitated, looking at my feet. His attitude seemed to have changed rather quick. Was it the dress or did he actually feel bad about yesterday?

"C'mon."

I couldn't do it anymore. "I thought you were done with me," I blurted, looking across the street into the darkness where I'd rather be.

Shaw sighed sharply and slid his hand onto my waist, pulling me close. "Does this look like I'm done?" His other hand found its way to the small of my back, preventing me from shoving him away. He gave me no choice as he pulled me into the crowd.

Placing my hands on his shoulders, I was hyper-aware of his body against mine as he moved me back and forth to the music. The one place I was fighting against and the only one I wanted to be in.

He leant his cheek against my hair and his chest rose as he breathed in deeply, tightening his grip on me. I closed my eyes, dipping my head into the crook of his neck. What was happening? I didn't understand what he wanted from me. I'd never been so confused in my entire life.

When his lips brushed against my ear, I shivered, stiffening in his grasp. It was too intimate after everything that had happened since the scout.

"About yesterday," he whispered, but I didn't let him finish.

"Please don't."

"Prue, I'm..."

"Whatever," I interrupted, pushing him away with the flats of my palms. I didn't want to hear an excuse. I knew what he would say and I didn't want him to break my heart anymore than he had. I just wanted to get through life without having that constant pain anymore. It had been a nice feeling dancing with him, but that was it. The end. It wouldn't happen again.

Turning away from him, I caught Eva's eye and her expression was anything but friendly. If looks could kill, I'd be deader than dead. I'd be ash. Great, just what I needed. A vendetta from the Mayor's daughter.

"Wait," Shaw said behind me, but I just waved him off, walking through the crowd of people, finally stopping by the table of drinks Hannah and I had set up before.

I took a cup to busy myself and looked back to see if I could see her and there she was dancing with Bobby. She winked suggestively at me and I smiled back. At least one of us was having a good time.

"She's like a wild thing, you know?" Eva's annoying voice was a little louder than it should be. I afforded one glance to confirm what I knew was true. She was standing with her back to me, a group of women around her. Faces I recognized from around town, but whose names I wasn't sure of. Amy was with them and she glanced at me, her expression uncomfortable. She wouldn't stand up to Eva, but who gave a shit what they thought?

"Who knows what she was doing out there," another woman was saying.

"What was she eating?"

"Do you think she killed anyone?"

"Yes. I know she did."

This seemed to stifle them for a moment, but I refused to listen anymore. To them, I was just the wild woman of the waste. Like the wicked witch from the Wizard of OZ. These women didn't know what survival was. They had been lucky when luck didn't exist and I hated them for it. Most of all perfect, beautiful Eva Thompson. I wanted to teach her a lesson, but it wasn't worth the effort. One day she would have to step up and would be found wanting.

Truth was, she was trying to get me out of the picture so she could sink her claws deeper into Shaw. It was a childish bully tactic and it looked like it was working. But, she didn't need any help. I'd done all the leg work on my own. I would end up being on the outer with everyone and she would get exactly what she wanted.

I looked back across the street where Shaw was talking to some of the other guys who worked on the wall. Other than Hannah, he was the closest thing I'd had to a friend in years and I hated to admit it, but his opinion had come to matter to me. He'd seen the person this world had forced me to become and it was glaringly obvious that he didn't like what he saw.

I looked away before he could catch me staring, running my eyes over the group of people that I'd come to know. There was close to eighty or ninety people who lived here, and it felt like a throng. Everyone was here, even the kids. My chest constricted and I took a deep breath. I'd never had a panic attack or anxiety, but I imagined that this was how it'd feel. Oxygen wasn't getting in, despite the deep breaths I was taking.

Putting the cup back on the table, I turned and walked away down the street, away from the lights and the noise, every step taking me closer to freedom. Or that's how it felt as I began to breathe normally again.

I'd never been around that many people at once since

Quarantine and after everything with Shaw and his abrupt change in demeanor and Eva's bitchiness… it was just too much. So, I just walked in the darkness and the quiet where I could be alone without the threat of discovery looming over my shoulder. I was safe in the town. I snorted. That wasn't quite right… I was safe from death at least.

It felt better out in the darkness.

I found myself down at the farm, outside the milking shed and I eased my way inside. The smell of cows and hay had become familiar over the past few weeks, or was it months, and almost felt calming. The two old heifers were in their pens at the rear of the shed, their shuffling audible over the dull echo of the party. I lent over the stall door and offered a handful of hay to the one I had begun to think of as Bethel. A name perfect for an old lady.

I couldn't deny that I had thought about leaving. Life here was too complicated and all these people and feelings were overwhelming. Someone once said that to let in the good you also had to let in the bad. They waked hand in hand no matter where you went. But in this world, the bad was pretty bloody bad.

There was a rustling sound from behind and I turned instinctively, my back flattening against the door, Bethel lowing in fright.

"Sorry." It was Shaw.

I sighed sharply and shook my head. What was he doing here?

"Sorry," he said again. "I should know by now not to sneak up on you."

I didn't like being followed. Not even by Shaw. "What do you want?"

"You left rather suddenly, I was worried." He was frowning. I knew I confused him more often than not, but I wasn't used to this. A man being so attentive one moment, distant the next. I wondered when he would tire of it.

"I'm okay," I said more to appease him than actually meaning it.

An awkward silence fell then and I sat down on a bale of hay and waited. He'd dumped the pretty mayor's daughter to come and talk with the deranged wild woman of the waste. He was looking at the ground, arms crossed and I wondered what he was thinking. Suddenly, I really wished he hadn't of followed me here. It would be better if he stayed at the party with Eva. She was vapid, but at least she was normal. I was screwed in the head.

He sat down on the bale next to me a little too close for comfort, I could feel the warmth radiating from his body in the cool air. I looked down at my hands and was suddenly very aware of how short the dress was that Hannah had given me.

"I never thanked you," Shaw said, playing with a piece of straw. Even though it came out a whisper, it startled me.

I looked up at him in the darkness, his eyes glittering in the moonlight. Fuck it all to hell, I cursed to myself and was thankful he couldn't see me blush.

"You don't need to thank me," I said to cover my sudden shyness.

All I could think about was his hands on me. I wanted to kiss him so damn much it ached, but I jammed those thoughts back to the dark corners from whence they had came. I didn't want to feel those feelings. In this world, it didn't seem possible. None of it. I had to get out of there. I steeled myself to stand and walk away, but he spoke again.

"I'm sorry about yesterday."

I shrugged.

"I didn't mean to hurt you."

"You didn't."

He let out a slow breath and shook his head. "Yeah, I did. I should have just talked to you about it. I was a jerk."

I didn't say anything. If I did, he would know that I was trying to hold back tears. He was silent for a while, which gave me time to compose myself.

"You saved my life," he said quietly. "And I acted like a stupid fuck."

I could understand why the whole thing would have been confronting, but I still killed a man in front of him.

"Did you ever see anyone else out there?"

His question kind of surprised me. He'd never pushed me to talk about before and I never wanted to talk about it, but I answered anyway. "Yes."

"Like who?"

"Thieves, rapists, murderers." Who else was there?

"Were you ever attacked by any of them?"

"Yes."

"Were you..." He couldn't say the word rape.

"No."

He was visibly relieved. "What happened to the ones who attacked you?"

"I killed them before they could kill me."

He dropped his head into his hands as I knew he would.

"Do you think I'm a monster?"

His head snapped up and he stared at me, eyes glittering. I couldn't tell what he was thinking, but I could guess. My heart sunk.

"You do." It was a statement.

"No," he was shaking his head. "Prue, I don't think you're a monster. You did what you needed to survive."

"Have you ever killed anyone?" I didn't know what tact was anymore.

Shaw stood up abruptly and paced back and forth, his hands running through his hair.

"Sorry."

"Prue," he hissed. "Fuck."

I looked at my hands, trying to block out his form in front of me. "I don't belong here."

"Prue…"

"They all think I'm deranged and maybe I am."

"Those women have never seen a hard day in their life. This is as hard as it's got. After everything you've been through, you're the one who deserves to belong here."

I shook my head, not trusting myself to answer.

Before I knew what was happening, he pulled me to my feet, arms winding around my waist and his lips found mine. I had forgotten what it felt like to be kissed. Any memory I had was burnt away by the feel of Shaw's tongue against mine. He kissed me like he was starving. His hands caressed my back, pulling me hard against the length of his body. Impulsively, I let my hands run through his hair, my fingers winding into his messy locks. I instantly regretted it, but I couldn't stop myself. I wanted him.

The feeling of his lips on mine, his smell, his taste, it overwhelmed everything else and I could almost forget everything that had happened. He still wanted me after he'd seen me do that awful thing that had saved his life. I felt it in the entire length of his body and the tender way he held me to him.

Shaw's kiss became deeper and I couldn't hold back a moan of pleasure when his hands found the bare skin of my thighs. Fingers lightly trailed over the jagged scar that had forced our meeting and I shivered.

He drew back, eyes searching mine. "Are you cold?"

I shook my head, my hands falling to his broad shoulders. I had almost become used to the fact that he thought I was a monster, but here he was kissing me. I wanted to run before it was too late. But it already was, wasn't it?

"I'm not done," he whispered, cupping my face. "You scared the hell out of me, but I'm not done."

I couldn't say anything. Whatever strangled response I was trying to think of died in my throat.

He brushed his lips lightly against mine and whispered, "I should say goodnight."

I nodded, like a deer mesmerized by the headlights of an oncoming truck.

"Thank you," he murmured.

"For what?" I managed to get out.

"For telling me."

I swallowed hard and nodded, extracting myself awkwardly from his arms. I knew he was looking at me with some semblance of a hurt expression, but I couldn't bring my eyes up from the ground. It was like I was fifteen again, running away like a scared little girl who'd gotten in too far over her head. But, that's exactly what I did and Shaw didn't try and stop me.

Thirteen

I was scared.

I was scared every single day that this would be the end. That every step I took would take me closer to a horrible death. I was so scared I hardly knew why I wanted to go on living.

The bush loomed around me, dulling my footsteps through the ferns that covered the ground like a carpet. The air outside would be warm and fresh, but in here it was close and suffocating. Cover was good and open was bad. Down the bottom of the gully was a creek, I could hear it trickling through the trunks of the gums. It sounded close, but I knew that sound had a strange way of distorting in the forest.

There was movement ahead and I slowed, eyes focused on a shadow in the distance, hoping it was just a wallaby or a kangaroo. I'd seen plenty of those in the last few days. But the shadow moved fluidly and I knew something wasn't right. It wasn't an animal, it was *human* and by the build, it was a man.

I came to an abrupt standstill, my eyes locked on the man in the distance. When he stopped just as suddenly, I knew he was looking right back at me and my breath caught. There was a sharp whistle on the air like a bird call, and somehow I knew that it hadn't come from a bird. An answering call echoed through the bush behind me and my heart almost completely stopped as the sound petered out.

There were two of them.

I only had one option. Without breaking stride, I ran headlong down the gully, branches and leaves snapping and cracking underneath my feet. In an instant, there was the sounds of pursuit. The man that had been to my left and the second person that I now knew had been behind.

My foot snagged on a hidden branch and I pitched forward, landing on my shoulder and rolled several feel down the incline. Before I could scramble back to my feet, I was set on from behind.

One of the men was on my back, tearing my pack and sword away, grinding my face into the hard clay ground. I felt the sting of rocks cutting into my skin, but there was nothing I could do about it. I was turned over roughly and for the first time I looked right into the eyes of my attackers and it wasn't pretty. They were both dirty and thin, their hair matted and their clothing looked like it had never been washed. They both stunk like old urine and I couldn't help it when I gagged.

One set of hands held my feet and the man who straddled me, held my wrists above my head. So, this was how it was going to go and I wasn't going to make it easy. I bucked and jerked against them, trying to head-butt the man on top of me, but his weight held me down and made me feel sick.

Dirty hands were grabbing at my pants, trying to pull them down as I struggled. A foot came free and I brought my knee up hard into the man's groin and he fell on top of me with a surprised grunt. Shoving him off, I kicked out at the other man before he could grab my foot, clipping him on the jaw.

By some miracle, I was free. Scrambling backwards, my hand landed on the hilt of my sword as both men advanced, but I didn't hesitate. Hesitation meant I was the one who was going to die at the end of this. The sharp ringing of metal split the air and I swung with a practiced aim. Steel hit flesh, followed by a dull thud as the first man went down. The second stopped, his eyes wide as blood soaked into the ground around his friend.

By the time he had gathered his thoughts, I was on my feet. He turned to run, but I was already bringing down the sword. I'm sure it wasn't intended to be used this way, the blade was way too long, but the steel imbedded into the man's back into where I supposed his heart might have been, had he had one.

Yanking the sword free, I picked up the sheath and my pack, donning both again and ran down the gully.

Any emotion I might have felt, I had learned to shut off. I'd turned my back on that part of myself a long time ago and now I was incapable.

Incapable of love. Incapable of feeling. Incapable of mercy. Incapable of remorse.

I dreamed all the time. Mostly I forgot the specifics, but never what they were about. This time, I remembered everything. Because this dream had been true.

I was incapable of so many things, it was a wonder I could still function. It was a wonder I could have a broken heart when I obviously didn't have one.

I sat on the wall, the mid-morning sunshine hot on my back as my eyes ran over the bush, the dream playing on my mind. The shadows were flung backwards by the light, but it didn't stop my eyes playing tricks on me. Residual images from the night hovering in the tree line. Every time I straightened up, I realized I was just seeing things. Wind in the brush. A flock of parrots in the branches of the ghost gums. I began to doubt my usefulness.

I knew Shaw was walking today, but I hadn't seen him yet. He'd put himself on the line, put his feelings right out there and I'd just run away. I just kept hurting him no matter what I did. I had a decision to make and I felt like I'd be a loser whatever way it went. I couldn't think about myself like a selfish child. I had to think about what was best for Shaw.

When he inevitably passed my position he ignored me, but I didn't expect anything less. My thoughts were plagued with images from the scout and the party. His hands on my waist, in my hair. His lips on mine. But it all ended with that scene in the bush. Blood on his face and the shock he'd sunk into.

How did I become so fucked up? Oh yeah, spending three years in the bush with no one but myself and the occasional rapist and mutated monster might have something to do with that. My life before had a great deal to do with making me into this. I was a very angry person and that had never really gone away. My only experiences with relationships were bad ones and I had been used by so called friends too many times to count. I'd stopped trying a long time ago. The end of the world was the end of any possibility for light and love for me. It was the final nail in the coffin.

I was just existing. Going through the motions. And then there was Shaw. Losing him had hurt me more than anything else since the world had died.

I hadn't seen Hannah in a few days, so after I was done on the wall, I went round to her house. She had been such a good friend to me and I needed to see a happy face.

She flung the door open a second after I knocked and smiled brightly through the wire door. "Come in," she said, pushing it open. "What's up?"

"Just coming for a visit," I said, walking into the cool air of the old house. "I haven't seen you for a few days."

"Not since the party," she winked, leading me to the kitchen "Water?"

"Please."

"Did you have a good time? What did you think of it?"

"The party?" I sighed. "It was okay, I guess." It was shit actually, but I wasn't about to hurt anyone else's feelings over it.

"You don't sound so convinced, Prue," Hannah nudged me with her words, filling a glass to the brim with water from the plastic container on the countertop.

"Eva was less than nice."

"But what's new, right?" Hannah rolled her eyes. "If you want me to say something…"

"No," I shook my head. The last thing I needed was trouble after what Shaw had told her.

"Is everything okay?" she asked, handing me a glass of water. "You seem more quiet than usual."

I shrugged. "I don't know."

"Did something happen? With Shaw?"

I looked up at her, my eyes wide.

"You disappeared during the party. Shaw was gone as well."

"Stop it," I whispered. I didn't want to tell her. I mean, I knew I was being stupid, but I didn't want her to think it.

"Did something happen?" she asked again, her voice full of concern.

What was I supposed to say? "He kissed me and I ran away like a scared little girl."

Hannah's face fell into relief, like she expected me to say something much worse. "You've nothing to fear from Shaw. He's a good guy."

"It's not me who should be afraid. He's got everything to be afraid about when I'm around."

"Prue, that's not true."

"I'm broken, Hannah. I'm so broken I can't be fixed. The things I've done…" I bit my lip to stop myself from going any further.

"You did for survival." She finished for me.

I felt tears welling in my eyes and it was all I could do to keep myself under control.

"Prue, if something's the matter, if something happened, you should talk about it," Hannah said, sitting beside me. "Keeping it inside isn't helping anyone."

Shaw never told anyone what happened. He never told anyone about that man and what I did. Not until Eva and she used it against me.

"It'll eat you alive until there's nothing left. Please, Prue."

She didn't seem to care. I mean, it seemed easy. Just to stand there and do it. Shaw's words flashed through my mind, mirroring Hannah's. There was nothing inside. Maybe that's what was wrong with me.

I stood abruptly. "I'm sorry, Hannah."

"Prue."

"I can't. I'm not ready." What I didn't want to admit was that if I was going to confide in anyone, I wanted to confide in Shaw. I wanted to tell him everything, but that chance was lost.

"It's okay," she said, standing to face me. "When you're ready, know that I'm here. Without judgment."

"Thank you."

She came around the edge of the table and wrapped her arms around me.

"I need to go help Nan," I said, extracting myself.

"Okay. But, take care, okay? I want to see you happy, Prue.

I want to see you smile."

"I'll try." And for the first time, I actually believed myself.

On the way back to Nan's I thought over everything that had happened since arriving at the town. I had a lot of shit to work through and Hannah was right in so many ways. I had to talk to somebody. I had to get over the fact that I had done bad things. Everyone already kind of knew that's what I might have had to do to survive this long. It was the part where I actually admitted it and let someone inside all the walls I'd built to protect myself that was the problem.

I worried my bottom lip. I wanted Shaw, but I didn't know how to fix it.

When I finally walked into the kitchen, Nan was already over the stove, cooking up a storm.

"Hello, dear," she said brightly, stirring a pot of something she was sprinkling spices into.

"Can I help?" I asked, but at the last second my voice wavered. Nan was always quick on the uptake, so when she turned around it didn't matter how schooled my expression was, she knew.

"Is everything okay?"

"Yes."

"Are you sure, Prue?" Nan asked gently.

"Yes."

She set down the wooden spoon that she had clutched in her hand and walked over to me. "I know you have dreams, dear. I hear you in the night. Are you sure you don't want to talk to someone about it?"

Nan had been so nice to me, but I couldn't tell her. "I

can't."

"Prue, sweetheart. It's eating you from the inside." Hannah's words.

"Please don't make me tell you."

"I won't make you do anything."

"I had to do it," I blurted. "I had to do horrible things. He was going to kill... I had to…"

"Oh, Prue," Nan cried, pulling me into her arms. She smelt like rose water and wood smoke from the fire.

She had that effect on me. The one where she was more like my mother than the lady who I lived with. The feeling of her arms around me finally coaxed those annoying tears to fall from my eyes and she rubbed her hands up and down my back.

"I'm sorry," I said through sobs.

"It's okay, dear. Crying is a good thing."

I knew she was right, but I'd always seen it as a weakness. It was hard to let go.

"Do you want some stew?" she asked, pulling back. "I managed to sneak some beef from Grace at the shop."

I nodded, wiping my eyes and Nan sat me down at the table and began fussing over the stove.

"Don't you worry about a thing, Prue," she said, filling a bowl. "I'll take care of you for as long as you'll let me."

And god, did I hope that was true. What I didn't say was that I'd do anything for her, too.

Fourteen

That night, I slept straight through for the first time since arriving in the town. And for the first time it was empty. No dreams plagued me and my eyes opened into clarity. It was a start, but there was still a long way to go.

Today, I was determined to go and speak with Captain Wallis. The trust was gone between Shaw and I and he had to be made aware of it. If he made me go out into the bush again with him on a scout, it could end in disaster. I had to tell Captain the truth.

It was still early, about seven am I guessed, and the streets were quiet. The kids were due at school at nine, whoever was on at the shop wasn't opening until eight and the farm was down the opposite end. It was quiet, the air hazy with a light mist. It wouldn't be long now until we had to go out and plant the crops for winter. Autumn was in full swing and it was a relief from the blazing heat of summer and this year, it had been longer than usual.

Rounding the corner, I saw Hannah at the end of the street, right by the cottage we used for as a guard house, the one where I'd heard all those things... and I stopped dead in my tracks. She was talking to Shaw. My heart instantly spasmed and I took a step backwards, all those things I'd started to work through jumbling together. I hadn't counted on this being my reaction. At this distance I couldn't tell what they were discussing, but I could read their expressions clear as day.

Hannah looked worried, her hands waving wildly as she spoke and Shaw's head was low, eyes on the ground. Taking a deep breath, I stepped forward, continuing on to my destination. The cottage they stood out the front of. As I came closer, Hannah looked up at me, her face turning red. So, I guess that meant they'd been talking about me. I couldn't bring myself to look at Shaw yet.

"Prue," came Hannah's voice, but I didn't want to hear any explanations. I knew why she was there and I was grateful, even though it might have been the wrong thing to do so soon after everything.

"I'm looking for Captain," I said, trying to make my voice sound confident and clear.

"He's in the kitchen." Shaw didn't sound like himself. The self that had become short with me and I knew that Hannah had let slip the comment I'd made about him being the one who should be afraid of me.

I wanted to see Captain even more now. If I had to go out there again, I wanted it to be on my own. If I was paired with Shaw, I wouldn't be able to handle it.

I made myself look up at him, but he was looking at the ground and suddenly our roles were reversed. "Thank you."

I found Captain in the kitchen, a book in his hand and a cup of tea in the other.

"Captain Wallis?" I asked, my voice loud in the silence.

"Oh," he said looking up from his book. "How's things, Prue?"

"May I speak with you? It's important."

"Of course," he smiled, nodding to the chair opposite.

I sat down, wringing my hands. "I know I've only been out once with Shaw, but I wanted to know if I could scout solo."

"Prue," he frowned and I knew he was going to argue against.

"I'm used to being on my own."

"Yes," he rubbed his chin. "I suppose you are. But, Shaw knows you better than the others and he can learn a lot for you. Your experience out there is invaluable."

"But, sir..."

"Prue, I understand, I do. After all you've been through, it's a wonder you haven't asked me earlier. But you've only been out once with Shaw and that was extremely beneficial. We wouldn't know about those creatures if it wasn't for you. Look, leave it a couple more weeks, then I'll think about it." He said it with a finality that dissuaded further argument. "I'm glad you brought him up, Prue. Shaw, I mean."

"Why's that?" I asked, my heart skipping a beat.

"Did something happen out there that you haven't told me? Shaw has been distant ever since you came back and I'm beginning to worry. It's totally out of character for him."

"I-" This was the reason I'd come here, but I still had trouble explaining it.

"We're going out to plant in the fields in a few days. I need to know if he will be okay. I don't want to send him out again on his own until I'm confident he will come back alive."

I needed to step up and take responsibility for the things I'd done. I needed to confide in somebody. Hannah was right about it eating me up. I'd been struggling with it ever since that day Shaw brought me here. Until that day, I didn't have to come to terms with the things I'd done. It was just the way life had become. It didn't have to be that way anymore and that's where the problem lied.

First, I needed to tell Captain about what happened with Shaw out in the waste. It was obvious he was struggling with it and I doubted talking to Eva was enough. He mightn't want to talk to me after everything, and I'd probably already lost him for good, but he had to talk to somebody. He hadn't told me, but I knew he respected Captain Wallis.

"Shaw didn't tell you the entire story about our scout. Something else happened and I'm worried about him."

"Why are you telling me this now?"

"I trusted he would come to you about it when I was gone."

"And he never spoke to you about it."

"We're not on good terms anymore."

"Go on," Captain said, folding his arms on the table.

"The second night we made camp at Shaw's usual spot. I went to check the perimeter. When I came back, I saw a man come from the opposite side of the clearing. I managed to circle round the back of him, but he had a gun to Shaw's head." I hesitated, my voice breaking.

"It's okay, Prue. What happened then?"

"He was going to kill him," I reasoned. "I had to. I got the gun from him and..." Captain frowned, not unkindly, but enough for me to not explain exactly how it went down.

"You have nothing to fear from us, Prue. Whatever you say to me will be between us. No one else."

Captain Wallis had been nothing but nice to me since the day I'd met him. I wanted to believe him so much.

"I cut his arm off, then I slit his throat."

"Shit," he hissed, running a hand over his face and I flinched, casting my eyes onto the table top. "No one will ever understand what you went through," he said, taking me by surprise. "No matter how you did it, you saved Shaw's life."

"Did he tell you how his Dad died?" It was out of my mouth before I knew it and I suddenly felt sick for betraying Shaw's trust.

"No. Do you think it has something to do with his reaction?"

I bit my lower lip, wondering if I went too far. "I think it was the same."

"Bloody hell."

"He won't talk to me, but he should talk to someone," I said, standing up. Captain looked at me for a long moment and I was scared he was going to say something about what I'd done. That they were going to make me leave and go back out there.

"Thank you, Prue," he said softly, the kindness in his voice taking me by surprise. "Thank you for confiding in me."

I looked at him wide-eyed and let out the breath I didn't realize I'd been holding in. Nodding, I left before he could change his mind.

I stood on the edge of a long forgotten country back road and squinted my eyes at the horizon.

The bitumen was crumbled and full of potholes and every so often I'd stumble into one with a curse. In the distance I saw Bobby coming the other direction having just as much trouble.

Almost everyone was in the field just outside town, busy planting the new crop for the winter. Wheat, chickpeas, oats, barley and canola. A mixed bag, but the more diverse the planting, the more options there were for all kinds of food. Wheat was the main one. Without it there wouldn't be bread.

I was walking the perimeter, along with nine others from the wall, making sure nothing went wrong. Under one arm I had a rifle and across my back was my sword. The gun felt heavy in my small hands, but it was necessary. One of the guys had shown me how to shoot. I'd never fired a gun before, even though I'd found a few over the years. All I knew was how to pull one apart and where the safety was. I preferred the silent and deadly approach.

Bobby gave me a high five as we passed on the road.

"Anything?" he asked.

"Nope."

"That's how we like it," he grinned, waving as we parted ways.

I'd felt a little better since I'd let out a few things. Telling Captain the truth about what happened out in the waste had let a load off and I hoped Shaw had taken it well. I hadn't seen him and he hadn't sought me out. I wasn't expecting him to. I just hoped that he would come to terms with everything that had happened out there. He didn't deserve to be broken. The town needed him more than it needed me.

I continued across the southern end of the field, turning when I got to the end. Facing north, I saw another figure in the distance. Instantly, I recognized Shaw. I'd know him anywhere. His stature, messy hair and the way he held his rifle. I'd taken more notice of him than I'd realized, my now misplaced attraction good for nothing but being able to recognize him from a distance.

I watched him approach as our footsteps brought us closer and by the look on his face, I knew that Captain had spoken to him. Whatever he was about to say to me wasn't going to be good. Perhaps in time he'd see that I was trying to help him.

He stopped in front of me, knuckles white around the butt of his rifle. "I know you told Captain behind my back." He ran a hand over his face, sighing loudly. He was pissed off and I didn't know what he was going to do.

Gritting my teeth, I said, "You talked to Eva about it. You would never talk to me."

"I would have talked to you about it, given time. I would

have talked to you about *everything.*" He spat the last word at me with such anger, I visibly flinched away from him.

"I didn't understand," I whispered. "I'm not...." I couldn't say the word 'capable'.

"Don't worry, Prue. I didn't count on it either," he snarled, looking away.

I wasn't going to stand there and take it anymore. Everything I seemed to do was wrong and everything I tried to do right... Well, that was just a joke. I spun on my heel and walked away, the gravel of the old road crunching under my feet.

"That's just great," came his voice behind me. "Running away again."

Anger flared in the pit of my stomach and before I knew what I was doing, I turned around and strode right up to him and shoved him hard in the chest. The last time my hands were in that position, he'd just kissed me. He stumbled back, a look of absolute surprise on his face.

"Do not talk to me about running," I spat. "I killed a man to save your life. I killed more to save myself. I'm fucking monster. I didn't want you to see it, but I had to make a choice. And I fucking chose you. I'm sorry I ran away, but I don't know how to deal with it. I'm broken, Shaw. I'm broken and I can't be fixed. Do you really want to deal with that for the rest of your life?"

He just stood there, staring at me dumbfounded.

"Thought so." I turned on my heel again and walked off, putting my mind back on the job.

"Prue," he called after me.

"I won't apologize for telling Captain," I said, coming to a standstill, my back still to him. "You should have done it yourself."

"Why didn't you call me out the day we came back?"

Turning around, I looked him right in the eye. I mean, this time I really looked. I couldn't be afraid of him anymore. He'd seen the things that I was afraid of showing, so there wasn't much left I *could* hide. The wasn't much left I could lose. Taking a deep breath, I said, "Because I was afraid I'd lose your respect. But, now I know that that happened the moment I saved your life. I didn't want to lose your friendship because I never thought I'd have that again. I thought I'd die out here alone. I told Captain because you don't deserve to end up like me."

Shaw stood there, looking at me with his strange green eyes and for a change, he was the one who couldn't speak.

Looking away with a sigh, I stood a few steps backward. When Shaw didn't make a move, I turned and continued down the road to the northern point of the field, my insides quivering so much, I thought I might have to bend over in the grass and throw up.

I had to be strong. I had so many things to come to terms with. The biggest one was admitting that I'd fallen for Shaw the day I'd seen him from Nan's porch. The first time I'd seen him since he'd saved my life. That's when it started. And I'd lost him for good; if I ever really had him in the first place and that was the mother load. I'd like to see a sane person deal with that.

Fifteen

It took three days for the crops to be planted and for three days I'd successfully avoided talking to Shaw. Captain had taken me aside the day I'd argued with him out on patrol and told me what I already knew.

Give it some time, Captain'd said. Time was a hot commodity and everyone was lining up for a slice.

Some time ago, Bobby had shown me how to clean the guns and today it was my turn to make sure everything was sparkling. He'd taken me through everything painfully slow, making sure I knew where the safety was and how to unload and check if there were any bullets in the barrel. I didn't have the heart to tell him that I knew what to do already, so I sat through his FAQ session in silence. It made him feel important, so I let him go.

Honestly, I found this kind of work calming. It was methodical, kind of like milking had been and I could focus on it without my mind wandering. And I was alone, which was the way I liked to operate. Like a ronin - a wandering samurai without a master.

When the door banged open, I automatically looked up and my heart clenched as Shaw walked in. He looked wild, a strange glint in his eyes and my hands instinctively tightened around the butt of the gun. I'd probably forever be frightened of shadows.

For a long moment he just stood there and didn't say anything, so I went back to work, putting the gun I was cleaning back together.

"I don't want to fix you," he said, his words hanging on the air like the preverbal elephant in the room. "I know I can't."

So, that's what had him worked up. Took his time.

"Then deal with it," I said. That's what I was trying to do.

"*Stop it.*"

"Look, Shaw. I made peace with the person I've become. I was fine with it when I was on my own."

"You're not now."

"No, but it's still my issue to deal with. And I'm dealing. On my own terms."

"Don't you understand, Prue?" He stood in front of me, hands on the table, but I still didn't look up.

"I understand completely."

"No, you don't. You don't have to do things on your own anymore."

"I'm not," I said, my fingers digging into the edge of the table.

"Then why won't you look at me?"

I clenched my jaw, trying not to grind my teeth. Sliding the chair back, I stood and raised my eyes to meet his. "What do you want me to say? Do you want to hear how I hid in a kitchen cupboard as a mutant scratched at the door hungry for my flesh? Do you want to hear about the time I was hunted through the bush and almost gang raped? How about the time I cut a man down in cold blood before he could stab me in the gut? How about..."

Shaw took two long strides around the table and pulled me against his hard chest, stopping me mid-sentence. "Enough."

I breathed in his familiar scent and almost caved. I was back in his arms and I didn't want to let go, but I had to. "That's who I am, Shaw. I can't feel anything, because how can you feel all of that?"

"I want to help you."

"I know."

"Why won't you let me?"

I should let him. He'd taken a lot of crap from me and after everything, he still wanted more. The kind of more that I couldn't do. When it came down to it, if I let Shaw in, I was afraid of dragging him down with me and breaking him, too. "I can't. It's too much."

"Look," he said, pulling away. "You don't have to tell me anything you don't want to. I won't force you to do anything you don't want... but please don't push me away. I know I did some shitty things and I'm sorry. I'm sorry about everything."

"I know. I just don't know how to give you what you want. I can't."

"Look, Prue," he said with a sigh. "I'm not going to

apologize for kissing you, I'd do it again... but you kissed me back. You can."

I stood awkwardly, clenching my fists.

"Just don't say never. Not now, I can do."

"Not now," I said, casting my eyes away.

He let me go with a sharp sigh, running his hand over his face. It was so quiet I heard the rasp as the stubble on his chin brushed against his palm.

"If I tell you about being out there... the things I had to do... I'm afraid it'll drag you down with me," I said quietly and pushed through the door before he could retort.

I needed to get away and think about it. Shaw overwhelmed me and when he spoke like that it felt like I was drowning. Maybe I could let him in, but right now it wasn't an option. Right now, I just had to get through today and when I could get through that, maybe then. I just needed some time. And that was something that everyone was hot for.

Lying in bed that night, I couldn't fall asleep. I had only just started sleeping in the bed again after weeks of sleeping on the floor. Every morning I'd get up and make the bed before Nan could see.

With the soft mattress against my back, I stared at the celling for the longest time, watching the shadows of the tree outside playing on the wall until finally, I got up. Pulling on my clothes and boots, I went outside and sat on the porch. It wasn't that cold, but I dragged on the kaki jacket that I'd been given at the shop and flipped the collar up.

I had all these dreams and fears and worries. My mind constantly ticked over, my eyes were always open even when I was asleep. I never really shut off.

I don't know when I'd decided it, but I would tell Shaw. I would tell him in the morning. I would tell him anything he wanted to know. Most of all, I'd tell him the truth. That night at the party, he'd laid everything out. It was time I did the same, no matter what happened between us next.

A quarter moon hung low in the sky and stars twinkled in their thousands, reminding me of what Shaw had told me the day out in the bush when he'd made me swim with him. *The sky is like a time machine.*

He'd done nothing to warrant my coldness. I certainly didn't mean it, but he'd done nothing but look out for me. Even when I could have killed him and ran, he still tried to help me. His reaction had been the natural one. Shock. He'd struggled and I'd just ran away from it when I should have done what he did in the beginning.

When I went to see him tomorrow, I hoped it wasn't too late.

Sitting in the darkness on Nan's porch, movement to my left caught my eye and my gaze automatically flickered to the opposite side of the street. A shadow moved along the fence line and I stilled, watching. The unmistakable form of a man materialized as he came closer and I frowned. Something wasn't right... When he stepped into the moonlight, he turned his head, scanning the street. I didn't recognize him, but that didn't mean anything. There were still people I didn't really know living here, but what unsettled me was the fact that he was keeping to the shadows. That and the shotgun he held under one arm. That's what gave it away. He didn't belong here, which only meant one thing.

Once he'd disappeared into the shadow of the next street, I slipped back into the house, grabbing my sword and went to Nan's room.

"Nan," I whispered shaking her shoulder.

"Prue?" she said groggily. "What's the matter?"

"We've been breached," I said calmly. "Stay in the house and barricade the door."

"What?"

"Please, Nan. I'm going to warn the others."

She stared at me with wide eyes and nodded. Then she reached over to her nightstand and pulled out a revolver from the top drawer.

"What?" she whispered. "I might be old, but I can shoot a can off a fence at thirty paces."

I lent over and kissed her on the cheek and slipped back out onto the front porch. It was silent, but that meant nothing. Where there was one, there would be more.

I knew Shaw lived the closest of anyone. I'd never been to his house, but I knew it was in the block of units on Watson Avenue and the rear fence backed onto Nan's street. Nothing moved and I was certain that the man had moved on, so I darted across the street silently and vaulted myself over the fence palings, dragging my feet the last meter.

They had to have been watching us. When we went out planting, they would have counted our numbers. Especially the rotating guard. They would know exactly how many people were on the wall now. The thought briefly crossed my mind that it might be the same group of people that I'd been moving away from the day before I met Shaw. To take the town, there would be a sizeable number. Maybe twenty or so, but there was no way of telling.

I knocked lightly on Shaw's door, but there was no answer. Trying the knob, I found it unlocked and cursed his stupidity. Walking right in, I disregarded everything but one thing. He was asleep on the couch of all places and hadn't stirred at my abrupt entrance. Kneeling beside him, I slapped a hand down on his mouth and he jerked awake, eyes wide. When he finally focused on me, he wrapped a hand around my wrist, puling my hand away.

"We've been breached," I whispered.

"What the fuck?" he hissed, sitting up. It was then I realized he was shirtless and I didn't think about that.

"I saw a man drop from the wall by Nan's. I didn't recognize him. There will be more."

"Where's Nan?"

"I told her to barricade herself inside."

"Good." He got to his feet and began pulling on clothes that he'd flung over the back of the couch. A second later, he picked up his rifle from against the wall near where his head had been.

"Warn Captain and get the guys. I'll scout them out."

"No, Prue, they could be lurking anywhere."

"I'm good at stealth," I hissed back at him. "We've no time to argue about this. Raise the alarm."

I went to leave, but Shaw grabbed my arm. "Be careful."

"Always," I said and pushed through the front door.

Circling back towards Nan's I scanned each street and yard, looking for the man I'd seen. Keeping to the shadows I made my way around the edge of town. It wasn't long before my fears we confirmed. Another shadow flitted through the houses in front of me and this one was different to the first man I'd seen. This one had a handgun and was wearing a baseball cap and was moving more sluggishly than his mate.

Enough time had gone by for Shaw to get to Captain and the guys currently on the wall. I knew all of them and they were the only ones who had access to the firearms. The man in front of me was a stranger. Ratty clothing, limp hair, thin stature and I could smell his stink from here. Loosening my sword, I pulled it free, the blade rasping against the sheath.

He turned, trying to find the source of the sound, but I was behind him in the darkness. Stepping up, I slid the blade across his throat and he stifled a surprised grunt.

"You don't belong here," I whispered in his ear, trying not to gag from the reek of his unwashed body.

He jerked his elbow back, trying to disarm me, but I was anticipating it. As I stepped to the side, I sunk the blade into his flesh and he dropped.

Stepping over him, I continued through the streets, combing for more intruders. I could have tried to capture him, but that would have been useless. The moment I dropped the sword, he would have smashed it from my hand and blown my head off. The decision was simple and one I'd made time and time again. Me or him.

I came across five more at various intervals around the

streets near the wall. And every time I cut them down like a ghost. They didn't hear me coming and they didn't put up a fight. This was the first home I'd had in years and I'd do anything to protect it and its inhabitants. I'd do all of those horrible things that made me a monster a million times over if it spared this place and the people I'd fallen for.

I stalked the streets with one single focus and thought of nothing else.

The sounds of a struggle drew my attention and I ran silently over the grass to the end of the alley that ran near the side of the Mayor's house. Leaning around the corner, there were two figures close to where I was hiding, one male and one very female. My breath caught as I instantly recognized Eva against the fence, one of the intruders pressed against her trying to rip at her clothes.

He had a hand over her mouth, but I could still hear muffled cries as she struggled against him. My skin crawled with a memory that was best left forgotten and no matter how mean Eva had been to me, she didn't deserve this. No one did.

Stepping out of the darkness, I approached silently, the man too intent on Eva to notice what was about to happen to him. Raising my sword, I slid it between them, right against the man's throat and he stumbled back in surprise. The tip of the blade followed him as he turned on me, eyes betraying his fear, but when he saw I was a woman, he let out a laugh.

"What's so funny?" I asked, cocking my head to the side. Out the corner of my eye, Eva scrambled away, huddling against the fence behind me.

"A bitch with a sword."

Something inside of me turned off and I brought up my left hand to grip the hilt. Swords like this required two hands for maximum carnage. The Japanese intended them to be used artfully and as an extension of yourself. Your *whole* self. Pulling the tip of the blade away from his chest, he went to lunge, but I was faster. Moonlight glinted off steel as I swung, a movement I was familiar with from the hours of kata I'd done out in the bush. A dance for calmness and strength was now a dance for killing.

The man slumped to the ground with a grunt as blood began to pool beneath him into the grass.

"Prue?" Eva sobbed behind me.

"He would have killed you when he was done."

"I know."

We stood looking at each other for a long, silent moment until Eva said, "Thank you."

I nodded sharply. "Where's Mayor Thompson?"

"Dad told me to run," she sobbed. "They've got them inside."

"Who?"

"Dad, Grace, Hannah. Amy too, I think."

Fuck. Not Hannah.

"I think they've even got some of the kids. Prue, we have to do something."

My blood ran cold and I grabbed Eva's hand. "Come with me."

"Where are we going?"

"To find Captain Wallis and Shaw."

"What…" she began, but I didn't let her continue.

"If I'm going to kill those bastards and get everyone out of there, then I'm going to need back up."

Sixteen

Rounding the corner, I spotted a group of men from the wall, Captain and Shaw among them. They were all armed and talking fiercely with one another. Dragging Eva behind me, I let out a low whistle. Heads swiveled towards us as we approached.

"Prue?" came Shaw's voice through the darkness.

"Yeah, its me."

"Who's that with you?" Captain asked.

"It's Eva," came her voice behind me, no longer the haughty high and mighty bitch she'd been, but subdued with fear. I'd never have a problem with her again after what I just did.

"The town is clear," Captain said as Eva launched herself into Shaw's arms, sobbing uncontrollably. "There were twelve men found inside the wall. We found a few bodies that I assume you took care of."

"Thirteen," I said, nodding at Eva.

Shaw's eyes widened. "What…"

"Prue saved me. He was going to…"

"Eva said they've got hostages?" I interrupted before she could say anymore.

"Yes," Captain confirmed. "In Brian's house."

"Did we lose anyone?" I asked, afraid of the answer.

Captain nodded. "Four men on the wall."

Shaw narrowed his eyes, his arms still around Eva. "Simon, Freddy, Fisher and Cameron."

My jaw clenched and I felt bile rising in my throat.

"How many hostages and how many of them?" I said through clenched teeth.

"Three of them. Four adults. Brian, Grace, Amy and Hannah. Three kids."

Seven hostages, three gunmen. Probably armed to the teeth, too.

Mayor Thompson and Grace Howard. Council members. Hannah was Doc's apprentice. Amy was Captain's daughter. They'd even snatched some kids. The fact that they had so many important people led me to believe that this was an inside job and apparently, everyone else had come to the same conclusion. What didn't cross my mind as fast as it should have was the fact that they all thought it was me. They thought I was responsible for this.

"Who's to say that she's not in on this?" one of the guys snarled, jabbing a finger at me.

"Shut the fuck up, Red," Shaw shoved his hand away.

"I'm going in there and finishing this," I said, my voice even. Of course they'd think it was me. Of course they would. I was the dangerous broken girl with the samurai sword.

"Prue," Captain began, but I eyeballed him.

"This I can do," I said. "You said there were three men holding them. Three is easy."

Everyone was staring at me like I was some kind of... I don't know what, but they were all staring at me.

"There's a manhole in the floor." Eva's voice sounded strange in the darkness. She was out of place amongst the men from the wall, but I admired her for staying. This could end badly if I failed.

"Where?"

"At the back of the house, you can get under the floor. There's a few missing palings under the porch where you can slide under. Straight ahead there is a manhole that opens out into the laundry. It's underneath a rug, so no one knows it's there. Turn left up the hall and the lounge is straight ahead."

"Prue, you don't have to do this," Shaw said, placing a hand on my shoulder. "I can go."

"Stop trying to protect me," I scowled, twisting out of his grasp. "I obviously have to prove to you fucks that I'm not to blame for this. I will get them out. *Alive.*" Glaring at the guy named Red, I turned my back and walked the opposite way down the street away from the Mayor's house. I couldn't approach front on, they'd see me. I had to get at the house from behind.

The back fence of the house was a long box hedge slightly

taller than I was. Watering the garden seemed to be low on the priority list in recent years, because the lower half was scraggly and most of the internal branches were dried out to wood. Nevertheless, I was able to crawl through and into the backyard. The back of the house was clear and I darted across the grass and flattened my back against the weatherboards underneath a window. Running my eyes along the length of the porch, I saw the dark hole that must be the way underneath the house Eva was talking about.

Taking a few deep breaths and listening for movement, I edged along the side of the house. When I got to the open side of the porch, I crawled the last meter and slid into the darkness. All I had to do was go straight ahead and I'd hit the place where the manhole should be, but the lack of light made it harder than I'd hoped. Taking off my sword, I rolled onto my back and slung it across my front. Sliding as silently as I could through the dirt and rocks that littered the crawlspace, I felt the underside of the house as I went, fingers brushing against wood, cobwebs and who knew what else. Once upon a time, I'd been scared of spiders, especially the huntsman's that used to find their way inside during summer. Harmless, but scary all the same. Now, there were bigger things to be afraid of.

My hand hit the underside of the manhole just as I was about to give up and start again. The edge of the board rose slightly and I eased it back down, trying not to make a sound. Night, more than any other time of day, seemed to carry sound more readily that the stealthy liked.

Sitting up as far as I could without hitting my head, I eased the manhole open, the edge of the rug coming into view. There was no way to see out into the room, so I had to take a gamble and hope that the door was closed or that no one was walking past while I was half inside. As I pushed upwards, I followed into a standing position, the rug sliding aside and revealing the room. It was a stroke of luck that the door was closed and I was alone in the tiny space. Climbing out, I dropped the manhole closed with the dullest of thuds and the rug went back in it's place.

Ear to the door, I heard sounds of people, but it was hard to tell which direction they were coming from. Someone was arguing and it probably wasn't good. Taking my sword off my front, I strapped the sheath to my back and readied the blade. Cracking the door open slightly, I peered out into the darkness of the hall, a warm glow coming from the left. The coast was clear and now the only way was forward. Edging down the hallway, I kept close to the wall, listening to the heated conversation that I knew was from the intruders.

"They're all fucking dead," one man hissed. "Who the hell are these people?"

"Prue." My heart twisted and I stopped mid-step. That voice was familiar.

"You're saying a woman took out thirteen men all by herself?" Another voice.

"I wouldn't put it past her." That was Greg. What was he doing here?

"You better just give up now," came Mayor Thompson's voice. Clear and calm like he had been that first day I'd met him. "They won't let you get out of here alive. It's over."

There was a hard footfall and then the sound of flesh on flesh. "Shut the hell up, old man."

Stepping forward again, I couldn't believe it. Greg was in on this? He was the one who'd betrayed the town? I remembered all those days I'd spent down the farm milking with him and even the day he'd talked to me after one of Eva's tirades. But, I couldn't dwell on it now. I'd have to take him alive. Captain would want to question him.

An unfamiliar man stood right inside the doorway, standing with his back to me and a shotgun under his arm. Things always became more volatile when guns were involved, so I'd have to be quick. Get them before they could squeeze their triggers. I hadn't been made yet, so the element of surprise was still on my side.

Peering into the room, my eyes fell onto a small girl in Hannah's arms. She had to be about two or three years old, so it had to be Sarah and Tim's daughter, Renee. Hannah had told me about them when she first met me, that Renee was the first baby to be born after Quarantine, but I'd never had anything much to do with them. Now, I was responsible for their daughter's life.

Hannah looked up and caught my eye, her whole body stiffening. Pressing my finger to my lips, she cast her eyes back down then when the men didn't catch on, she looked back up. Pointing to the man that stood just inside the door she nodded slightly and pulled Renne closer, stroking her hair. I knew she understood what I was about to do. Some things a three year old child shouldn't see.

At this angle, there was only one way this was going down. Angling the blade upwards, I didn't hesitate. Putting all my weight behind it, the blade sliced through the man's chest like soft butter, blood oozing through his clothes.

The room erupted into screams and before the other men could shoot, I tore the sword free and brought it down against the throat of the one I knew what the ringleader. Out the corner of my eye, Grace kicked out Greg's knee from under him and bit into the arm that held a revolver. A split second later, she held it to his head, hands trembling.

My eyes focused on the ringleader and I pressed the blade into his skin, drawing a light smear of blood. "Drop the gun or I'll cut your head off."

He held out both hands and the clatter of metal on the hardwood floors signaled he was now disarmed. The sounds of crying children was the only thing that broke the silence. I'd done what I said I would without a shot going off, but I was still far from done.

"Got it, Prue," Mayor Thompson said, dragging the firearm away.

But, I only had eyes for the man that I had up against the edge of my sword. Finally getting a good look at him, there wasn't much to it. Stock standard wasteland asshole. Smelt like shit, looked like shit, acted like shit. "What did you think you were going to do once you had some hostages? Bargain with us? Make us leave? How were you going to run this place once we were all dead?"

"Psycho bitch," the man spat and I shoved him back against the wall.

"What did he offer you, Greg?" I snarled, not taking my eyes off the ringleader.

"Prue, he has my sister. I had to… they were going to kill her." Greg was almost hysterical.

The man began to laugh, showing off rotten teeth through his ugly chapped lips.

"What's so fucking funny?" I asked, putting a little more pressure on the sword.

"We killed the bitch two seconds after he left. Squealed like a little pig."

"She'd dead?" Greg's face drained of all color and before Grace could stop him, he'd forced the gun from her hand and pointed it at the man's face and pulled the trigger.

At point blank range it was too horrible to describe. The kids began screaming and crying, Hannah and Amy huddling with them, covering their eyes.

As he dropped to the floor, I pivoted on my foot and brought my sword down to Greg's throat, hardly aware that I was covered in blood and god knows what else. "Drop it," I said, my eyes fixed on his, but he was looking down at the remains of the man he'd just shot, his hand shaking.

"Drop it," I yelled again and the gun clattered to the floor, Grace snatching it up. "On your knees."

As Greg sunk to the floor looking utterly defeated, Mayor Thompson stepped forward, rubbing his brow with the back of his hand. "That's enough, Prue."

"Sir, with all respect, we lost four guys from the wall. I'm not letting him go."

"Who?" Hannah stood up, her voice panicked.

"Bobby's okay. Go outside and get Captain," I said. "Get the kids out of here. Get them home."

She didn't argue and they led them from the house, all the while her eyes diverted from the remains of the invaders. Greg was crying, his entire body shaking with shock. A lot more people could have died. The kids could have been hurt. It was all his fault. They had his sister? Then he should have asked for help. Ninety lives for one was a poor bargain.

There were footsteps in the hall and then in the room and hands were on my shoulders, pulling me away.

"It's done, Prue." Shaw. "We've got him now. You can let go."

"Fucking hell," Captain hissed as he laid eyes on the carnage.

I stepped back, letting the sword fall away and two guys took Greg by the arms and dragged him from the house.

"This was because of Greg?" asked Red, the guy who'd tried to pin it on me outside.

"It's the truth." Mayor Thompson. "Prue had nothing to do with this. I wouldn't have believed it anyway."

I just stared at the floor, overly conscious of being covered in blood and dirt, my hand sticking to the hilt of my sword. Not to mention the bodies I'd left in my wake.

Mayor Thompson was in front of me, hands on my shoulders and finally I looked up. "Prue, you did a selfless thing tonight. We'll be forever in your debt."

"I need to go check on Nan," I muttered and wandered outside, hardly aware that everyone's eyes were fixed on me.

They thought I was selfless? Didn't I just do it to clear my name? Maybe, but deep down I knew I'd done it because I was already tainted with blood. No one else needed that on their conscious, not if it wasn't necessary.

Covered in blood and darkness, I wandered home. I needed to see if Nan was okay.

I needed to go home.

Seventeen

"Are you a ninja?"

The mid-morning sunshine dappled across Nan's front garden to where I sat on the front steps of the porch, warming my bare legs. Across the yard, I saw one of the kids poking his head around the fence. I'd never spoken to any of them, so when he ran up the path and sat next to me, I was surprised. I'd thought they'd be scared of me, considering what I'd done.

"No, I'm not a ninja."

"But you saved us from the bad guys." He kind of looked disappointed.

"What's your name?"

"Ben."

I smiled down at him, at least a little glad that someone was talking to me. "You understand what I did was bad, right?"

He nodded.

"Sometimes you have to do a bad thing to save people, but it still doesn't make it right."

He nodded again, wide eyed.

"I'm not a ninja," I bumped his shoulder with my arm.

"But you're pretty bad ass."

I stifled a laugh. "Thanks, but I don't think your parents want you to say swear words."

Ben's face reddened.

I looked up and realized we had an audience. "You better go," I said. "Shaw's listening and he might tell."

Ben looked across the yard and jumped to his feet, running the other way. "Not if he doesn't catch me first," he shrieked taking off down the footpath.

Shaw smiled after him, but didn't move. When his gaze fell back on me, he grimaced. I knew I wasn't going to like anything he had to say and there was only one way this was ending; in an argument.

"How's Nan?" he asked standing in front of me.

"She's okay," I said, looking at his feet. "She was shaken, but fussing over me seemed to help her nerves." Fussing over anyone who'd let her was her favorite pastime.

"Captain and Mayor Thompson questioned Greg an hour ago," Shaw said, sitting next to me.

"And?"

"Greg was the last person to come to the town before you. That was almost two years ago. He claimed that he was made to infiltrate the town long term because they had his sister hostage. They used him to gain intel on us and smuggle out food and other supplies. When they thought they were in a better position, they decided to attack. But, I don't think they knew what you were capable of."

"They don't know for sure if she's dead," I said, ignoring the last part of his explanation. "What if there's more of them?"

"Greg also said that there was about fifteen in the group. All men. We counted fifteen bodies."

"What about their camp?" I wondered if there were more recruits after two years. Fifteen sounded like a low number to take out the town with.

"Captain will be sending some scouts to check it out."

"Are you going? Do they want me to go?" I didn't mind. Those kinds of people deserved everything they got, especially if what they did to Greg's sister was true.

"No," Shaw shook his head. "I'm staying here with you."

"But-"

"But nothing, Prue. It's being taken care of."

I sighed sharply, annoyed at being sidelined. "Have you seen Eva?"

"No. Mayor Thompson said she's still shaken up. She's resting, which is what you should be doing," he frowned at me.

"I don't know how to rest."

"That, I believe," he laughed.

Our conversation dropped off into nothing and we sat there in uncomfortable silence. I'd decided to tell him about before, but after what went down last night, I didn't know how to broach the subject. The moment seemed gone, but Shaw did the work for me.

"You asked me that night at the party if I'd ever killed anyone."

"Shaw," I began to protest, but he put a hand on my knee, the contact silencing me mid-sentence.

"I told you I went to Afghanistan when I was in the army. We always had to be careful, I mean there was the threat of snipers, ambush, roadside bombs. Something or someone was always trying to kill you when you were trying to save someone else. I had mates who died and I struggled with that. And knowing I'd taken out insurgents didn't make it any better. No matter what the intentions of the so-called enemy were, what I did wasn't much better."

His hand was still on my knee, so I slid mine over his.

"So, yeah, I killed people in the name of freedom. You killed people in the name of survival. There might be a line there, but it's bloody blurry if you ask me. So, I know what it's like. To feel like a monster." He knocked his knee against mine. "I just wished you had of told me earlier. Then we could have saved all this bullshit."

"I'm sorry. I didn't want to dump my problems on you." I wrapped my arms around myself.

"You don't have to say you're sorry. I know."

We sat in silence for a while and Shaw seemed reluctant to move his hand from my leg. His thumb stroked up and down over my kneecap, sending sparks along my skin.

"Do you see this as your home now?" he asked.

"Yes." Nan was my second mother, Hannah was my best friend and Shaw was... I didn't know what he was.

"Took you long enough."

"I guess five months is a long time at the end of the world," I shrugged.

"Prue, it's not the end of the world."

I looked up at him like he was mad.

"The Quarantine was just the end of the world *as we knew it*. The world is still here. It's just different."

"What do you want to know?" I asked, studying the closest rose bush. It had been pruned down to a stalk, ready to grow back in Spring.

"I'm not going to question you."

"You wanted me to talk. I want to tell you, but I don't know how to say it."

Shaw breathed in deep and let it out in a long sigh. "Were you afraid?"

"I'm afraid every day."

"Even now?"

"Especially now."

"Why?"

"Because I know how easily it can be taken away."

"Where were you in the beginning? How did you get away?"

"The day Quarantine went down, I was at my flat. I'd just spoken to my Mum and Dad on the phone. Stupid I know, but I'd already packed a bag by the time the Quarantine Officers knocked on my door. I managed to get out the back and over the fence before they broke in. I went to my brother's place, but the doors and windows were already painted."

"Did you find out what happened to them?"

"No. The house was immaculate. Nothing was missing. Nothing but Jase and Meg. I can only assume that they were caught in the Quarantine."

"You said your sword was your brother's?"

"I took it when I went to find them and after that I went bush. At first, I struggled. Finding food, shelter. For weeks I was afraid to go to sleep because I wasn't sure if I'd wake up. There was a scary lack of people which didn't make things any better. When I did come across them, I avoided contact like the plague. I was set on so many times. I was almost killed, robbed, raped... Any bad thing you can think of, I probably escaped it. I don't have to tell you how. The last thing my Dad told me was, *Have faith. Keep going. Things will get better.*"

"And he was right." A strong arm wound around my back.

"I had to withdraw so much to get through it. To cope," I said. "I didn't think I'd see anyone good again. I didn't think I'd have this. You. Everyone. I believed I was going to die out there and I probably would have if you didn't try to shoot me. I was so tired. I was so tired, I was just going to lay down and die."

"Shit."

"Maybe that was half my problem." I slumped against him.

"What do you mean?"

"Deep down, I'd already decided I was going to die, so trying to live was harder for it."

"Fuck, Prue."

"I'm trying."

As he leant his head against the top of mine, I closed my eyes, relishing in the feel of him. My shoulders felt lighter, my heart warmer, my head clearer.

"What are they going to do with Greg?" I asked.

"I don't know. I guess there'll be some kind of vote."

"A vote?" I scoffed, sitting up.

"It's the fairest way."

"Maybe, but are they going to lock him up? Forgive him? He should be left out in the middle of the bush."

"We're not savages, Prue," Shaw exclaimed.

"No, but you can't clap him in irons for the rest of his life."

"We can't just slit his throat."

"They were attacking us!"

"Greg said they had his sister..."

"Maybe, but do you think what he did was any better? There were other ways to go about getting her back."

"True, but..."

"No buts, Shaw," I exclaimed. "The one thing I learnt about surviving in this piece of shit world is that there is no grey area. Not where your life is concerned."

"Then what would you do?"

Without blinking I said, "Take him out into the middle of the bush and leave him there."

"Not a chance," he sputtered.

"Let the police handle it. Let some judge pass down sentence. They're all dead, so *we* have to do something about it. He was responsible for the deaths of four innocent men."

"Killing him would be fucking cold. We're not dead inside."

I stiffened beside him and bit my lip.

"It's-" Shaw began, realizing what he'd just said.

"I'm cold and dead inside," I spat, rising sharply to my feet.

"That's not what I meant," he exclaimed, standing to face me.

"Don't worry about it, Shaw. I get it. You've seen everything I'm capable of and how could I be anything else."

"It came out wrong. I-"

"I'm not who you want me to be."

"And what do you know about what I want?"

"Eva wants you. Maybe you should be with her. At least she's normal."

"I don't want her, I want-" He stopped mid-sentence, grinding his teeth together.

"See?" I scoffed. "You can't even say it."

"Don't do this, Prue. Not after everything."

"Do what? You're the one who said all of those things to me, trying to make me give in to you. What for? So you could see just how fucked up I am? Want to hear a scary story? You've heard it all now. The entire fucked up thing."

"Calm down," he pleaded, but his words had opened a floodgate inside of me. A gate that had been shut for years.

"You don't want me, Shaw. You want the idea of me. Reality isn't what it's cracked up to be."

"Prue, please. Just listen to me."

"You said you didn't want to fix me. So, stop trying."

"Prue, for fuck's sake." Shaw grabbed my arm, trying to calm me down.

"I'm not a toy," I yelled, yanking my arm away. "I'm not a toy that you can stick back together."

"I don't know what to say to make you see..." The words died in his throat. "Everything I do seems to be wrong."

I let my head fall into my hands as tears fell from my eyes.

"I want you," he whispered. "Cracks and all. What do I need to do to get you to see it?"

"It's not my call," I whispered. "It's not my call what happens to Greg. I don't want to fight about it. I'm tired. I'm so fucking tired."

Strong hands were against my upper arms, running up and down and I let myself fall forward into Shaw's chest. He dragged me down to the porch steps again, grabbing my legs and pulling them across his lap. Strong arms were around me before I could protest. Giving in, I let my head fall to the crook of his neck and he let out a long sigh.

"You're a hard mountain to climb," he murmured into my hair.

"I don't mean to be."

"I know. I just want to see you smile."

We sat in silence for the longest time. For once in my life I was content to let him hold me and I cursed the fact that the world had to end before we were flung in each others paths.

"I really appreciate that you told me those things," Shaw

whispered, breaking the silence. "Your trust means the world to me." He covered my hands with his, the hard callouses on his palms rasping against my skin.

"Don't leave me," I whispered. "Everyone leaves."

"Never."

Eighteen

I could still hear the screams. Mine, theirs. It didn't matter. Lying in bed that night, it was all I could hear. When I finally managed to drift off into some semblance of sleep, it was that fitful in-between place; not awake, but not asleep. The mix of dreams and reality were so vivid it was hard to tell which way was up.

Everyone kept thanking me and I probably shouldn't have a hard time accepting that what I'd done was ultimately good, but it still weighed on my mind. Walking through the town cutting down men who would take everything and leave us cold. I didn't know how I should feel about it. We lost four men, but we could have lost everyone.

Greg smiled down at me with a sick look of triumph and I hated him. I actually hated him with the fire of a thousand suns. He'd done a bad thing out of desperation and had almost took everyone I'd come to love. Nan, Hannah, Amy... Shaw. I loved Shaw. And Greg still smiled down at me like some kind of devil in a nightmare I couldn't wake from.

My eyes snapped open and fixed onto a face that didn't belong here.

"Greg?" I was asleep. I had to be asleep.

When he sunk his weight on top of me, curling his fingers around my neck, I was instantly awake. So, definitely not a dream. I didn't know how to scream anymore, fighting was my thing these days, so I grabbed anything I could lay my hands on and tried to smash him in the head. The book I'd been reading and the useless lamp, but he didn't budge, even when I smashed a glass into his temple. His weight was pressing me into the mattress and I struggled desperately against him.

His fingers squeezed around my neck, crushing and bruising, every second cutting off more and more oxygen. "If it wasn't for you then I wouldn't be like this. A prisoner," he snarled into my ear. "How does it feel to die, Prue?"

"I didn't kill her," I rasped, clawing his hand. "Don't do this."

"You survived when she didn't."

Greg squeezed tighter with a manic glint in his eye, the friendly guy I'd met while milking gone. Black spots prickled my vision as I tried to fight against him, but he was too strong. Struggling was no use, I was becoming more sluggish as oxygen was being cut from my starved lungs. The sensation of my windpipe closing in on itself was otherworldly. It didn't seem real. After everything, this was how it was going to end?

And just as I thought I was done for, he was gone. I drew in sharp breaths, coughing and clawing at the sheets.

There was a loud crash and the sounds of flesh pounding against flesh. Rolling over, I realized someone had pulled Greg off me and was beating the hell out of him. My vision blurred and it was all I could do to hold on, but even in the darkness, I'd know Shaw anywhere. What he was doing here was a mystery, but I was bloody glad he decided to show up in the middle of the night. He could show up whenever he wanted.

Sinking back onto the mattress, I was hardly aware that Nan was shouting somewhere outside and that Shaw stood over Greg's inert body, his shoulders heaving. The coppery scent of blood on the air was the only indicator that Greg was...

"Shaw?" I rasped. He didn't... he couldn't have. Not for me.

His head snapped up and he was across the room in two strides, pulling me up off the bed and into his arms.

"God dammit, Prue. I thought I'd lost you." The stubble on his chin rasped against my forehead as he spoke. He held me so tightly I couldn't push away and he sniffed like he'd been crying. Why wasn't I crying?

There were voices and lights bobbing across the yard attracted by the commotion. Captain and Doc were in the doorway, their faces surprised as they took in the scene. Shaw clutching me like I was going to disappear, my wide eyed shock and a seriously bloodied Greg on the floor.

"Jesus H. Christ," Doc whispered.

Captain crossed the room in three strides and dropped down to check Greg's pulse. "Alive," he sighed. "Just." He sounded disappointed.

Doc was looking at Shaw with a concerned expression.

"You can let her go now, son."

He seemed confused for a moment, then slowly relaxed his grasp, his arms falling away, but I didn't want to let him go.

"Come on, love," Doc murmured to me. "Come out into the kitchen away from this."

Looking back over my shoulder as Shaw led me down the hall, I watched Captain drag Greg's unconscious body out the back, where Bobby was holding the wire door open.

Sitting in the kitchen, Nan put a pot of water on to boil, her dressing gown drawn tightly around herself, hair wild.

Doc Howard glanced over me. "I can fetch Hannah, if you want."

"No," I shook my head, my neck pulling. She'd been through enough as it was. "He didn't touch me like that. Just my neck."

Doc reached out gingerly and examined the marks that Greg's hands had left on my skin. He pressed his fingers around, trying to see if there was any damage I suppose. "It'll probably bruise a nice shade of black, but there doesn't seem to be anything lasting."

"Thanks, Doc."

"Oh, dear. I'm so glad," Nan cooed, sitting beside me at the table, taking me in her soft arms. "You gave us a fright."

"How did he get out?" Shaw hissed. "If I hadn't of..."

"Son, who the hell knows. That's for Wallis to work out. Right now, I'm more concerned about you two than fixing up his sorry behind. Let me see," Doc gestured for Shaw's hand, which he placed on the table top. It didn't escape anyone's attention that it shook a little too much. "You've cut your hand to ribbons, son." He dabbed a damp cloth from Nan's pot of boiling water over his bleeding knuckles making him hiss.

"Leave it," he pulled away, blowing on the broken skin. "It'll scab quicker with air on it." Shaw turned to me, his eyes searching mine. "Are you sure you're okay?"

"Yes."

Shaw's good hand found mine under the table and I took it. I didn't dare try and read his emotions, but he squeezed softly, which was enough for me.

"Watch that doesn't get infected," Doc scolded him. "That's a worse mess to be cleaning up."

"No, sir," he replied, but something told me he wasn't really listening.

"If you're sure you're all okay, I better go see if Wallis needs me." Doc pushed his chair back, the legs scraping across the lino.

"We'll be fine, Tom," Nan said, shooing him out of the kitchen.

Then I was alone with Shaw. When we were out the front on the porch, I was suddenly unsure. I stood at the top of the steps and he stood on the path between the rose and vegetable garden. He seemed reluctant to go and I didn't want to let him walk away. Not again.

"Why were you here?" I asked after a moment.

"I wanted… There was…" He couldn't get his words out.

"It's okay," I said. "I'm okay." If he didn't turn up when he did, then I'd be dead and who knew what Greg would have done next.

Shaw hesitated and ran his good hand through his hair.

"What?" It was eating him up. I had to know.

"I don't want to leave you. Not tonight."

I felt a twinge in my heart and said, "Then don't."

He stood onto the step below mine and slid his hands onto my waist. Not now was becoming more and more right now as he pulled my body against his, his head resting against my shoulder. My arms wrapped around him, hands resting against the muscles in his back and it felt *right*.

"I love you, Prue."

I froze in his grasp. He was looking at me expectantly, his eyes full of need. I wanted to say it. I didn't know how to say it.

"I know the world has shit all over you, Prue. It's shit over all of us. But this is true. It's right. If I can't love you, then what hope is there left in the world?"

If I didn't do something now, then this would be it. He wouldn't forgive me again. Saying something like this... no one could come back from this.

I placed a shaking hand on his cheek, letting my fingers trace the edge of his jaw. The rasp of the stubble that always seemed to coat his face was familiar... it was Shaw. It was how I saw him. A little unruly, strong and *male*. He let his head drop, resting his forehead on mine, his eyes closed tightly. When my thumb reached his lips, he drew a shaky breath. Dropping my hand away, I pressed myself forward, our bodies fitting together, his arms around me.

The whole world disappeared. All the ugliness, the hate, the death, the blood. It all went away. All that mattered was that I was here with Shaw.

For the first time in years, I let go. My hands snaked

around Shaw's neck and I pulled him towards me, his surprised gasp allowing me to kiss him the way I had ached for for weeks. His tongue was against mine and I couldn't get enough. I pulled him deeper and he groaned into my mouth, his hands hard against my back.

"Do you think Nan will mind if you have a boy over?" he asked, lips still against mine.

"I-" I hesitated, my breath catching.

"It's not like that, Prue. I want to. God, I want to. But not like this."

Running my hands down his arms, I linked my fingers through his and led him back into the house, my bare feet cold on the floor. In my bedroom, there were still spots of blood on the floor where Greg had been lying, but I didn't look. That I'd clean in the morning.

Shaw kicked his boots off and I couldn't help but watch as he pulled off his shirt and trousers. It was like that day at the dam, where we were both one layer away from nothing and all of those thoughts came back in one hot flush. Laying back in bed, he gestured for me. I laid down next to him and he pulled me close, arms enveloping my tired frame. Where before I would have felt suffocated, I only felt safe.

"You're not going to disappear are you?" he whispered into my hair.

"No," I replied, breathing in his scent. "Where would I go?"

His only response was to hold me tighter.

"Why were you really here?" I asked him again. "Was it to tell me..."

"I couldn't take it anymore after what happened. Knowing that you could be taken away from me at any moment… If I didn't tell you how I felt…"

Turning over, I ran my hands over his waist, relishing in the feel of his skin. "I'm glad you cracked."

"Fuck, I think I loved you since the day I carried you back here."

"Are you sure it wasn't when I kicked you in the balls?"

His lips curved into a lopsided smile. Tonight, I'd been the one who was attacked, but I suspected Shaw was the one who was hurting the most. I hadn't made it easy on him.

"I know you're not ready," he whispered. "But I'll wait. As long as it takes."

His lips were against mine and it was everything I'd ever wanted. Shaw was everything I'd ever dreamed of. If the world truly ended right now, I'd be happy.

Nineteen

A heavy weight pressed down on my body and I twisted around, my heart lurching painfully.

"Prue?" a sleepy Shaw murmured in my ear.

The thudding in my chest began to subside as I realized I was in my bed and it was his arms and legs tangled with mine that had made me feel so disoriented. I reached out for him, my fingers finding bare skin.

"Are you okay?"

"Yeah," I whispered, my voice still husky from sleep. "I was just a little… out of it."

"Sorry." His hands were combing through my hair against the pillow as I stared up at the ceiling.

"It's just…"

"Different. I get it."

Turning so I could face him, I said, "It'll just take a little time. It took ages for me to be able to sleep in a bed again."

"What do you mean?"

"I slept on the floor for weeks," I whispered, my eyes searching his. "After all that time, I'd forgotten what a mattress felt like. It wasn't right."

He pressed his lips to my forehead as sounds from the kitchen echoed through the house. "Sounds like Nan's up," he said. "Better go face the music."

My face split into a smile of it's own accord and it was a nice feeling. "I feel like she's going to ground me for sneaking a boy into my room."

"Nan's cool," Shaw grinned and sat up, rubbing his eyes.

When I rolled over and set my feet on the floor, my neck began to ache and all the memories of what had happened last night flooded to the surface. Shaw sat beside me as I massaged the skin like it would magically heal the rising bruise.

"Are you okay?"

"It's tender," I said, grimacing. "But, it'll be okay."

He wrapped his arms around me again, kissing my shoulder. "This is nice."

"What do you mean?"

"Sleeping next to you. Touching you. Kissing you."

"It's different."

He let out a laugh and he was so handsome it hurt to look at him.

"Shut up," I said, pushing away and went over to the closet, pulling out some clean clothes. "Get dressed."

"What if I don't want to?" he said, a hand on my arm. He

spun me around and pressed me back against the wall, covering my mouth with his, a hand in my hair. I slid my hands over his waist and underneath the hem of his boxers. Shaw could kiss me until the end of time and I'd never get enough.

"Prue," he moaned against my lips. "You better stop doing that."

"Then you better get dressed."

He pulled away with a sigh and began dragging on his discarded clothes. Once we were both decent, we went out to the kitchen hand in hand.

"Ah, there you kids are," Nan beamed as we shuffled to the table. "I'm making some toast and porridge. We all need a good meal after last nights excitement. How are you feeling, Prue?"

She didn't seem to notice that Shaw had stayed the night and if she did, she wasn't worried. "I'm a little sore, but I'm okay."

"You gave us a fright," she cooed, placing a plate of toast in front of us. "But, nothing can be done about that. How's your hand, Shaw?"

"Much the same," he said, glancing at me.

"I don't mind," Nan said, picking up on our confusion. "Prue deserves a little happiness after everything that's happened. But, I have one rule in this house. No *you know what*. Some things an old lady doesn't need to hear."

"Nan," I groaned, but she laughed and turned back to the stove.

"They're having a memorial for the boys today," she said. "Down by the church."

"Captain told me yesterday arvo," Shaw said. "After breakfast."

"It'll be tough. We've been lucky it hasn't happened sooner, to be honest. Though, it's sad to think that it should happen at all."

"It's the world we live in."

I glanced up at Shaw and he shrugged. Did I know about the world....

Nan picked up the pot of porridge and dropped it with a clang back on the stove top. She clutched the side of the bench, her hand over her chest.

"Nan?" I asked, going to stand.

"I'm okay," she waved me off. "Just a little ache, is all."

"Nan," Shaw said, getting up. "You go a million miles an hour. Come sit down."

As Shaw helped her to her usual chair, I retrieved the pot, spooning out a share of the porridge to everyone. Setting a glass of water in front of her, I said, "Have some water. I'll take care of breakfast."

"Thank you dear," she said and I couldn't help noticing how breathless she sounded. I knew Nan was in her seventies, but she always seemed so... strong.

My eye caught Shaw's and he frowned. "Do you want me to go get Doc?" he asked after a minute.

"No, no, don't be silly," Nan exclaimed. "Just a little flutter. Let me be."

After Shaw and I cleared up the dishes from breakfast, we walked over to the park next to the old church. One arm was through Shaw's and the other through Nan's and even though we were going to a funeral, I felt content. This was the place I was meant to be.

As soon as we arrived everyone went their separate ways, Shaw wanted to speak to Fisher's girlfriend and Nan wanted to check up on Grace and the kids. My eyes scanned the crowd of people that had collected in the park, searching for Hannah. I hadn't had a chance to see her, what with everything that had gone down since the breach. I wondered if she was okay.

"Hi, Prue."

I turned at the sound of Eva's voice and found her standing behind me, hands folded and shoulders slumped. I remembered the first day I'd met her, how high and mighty she'd been in her prefect dress with her perfect hair. Now, she looked defeated, like she'd finally understood what had happened to the world. I didn't feel sorry for her, for what had almost happened, but I understood. It'd happened to me.

"I just wanted to thank you," she continued. "For saving me."

"You're welcome."

"I'm sorry I was such a bitch. I mean, I didn't make things easy for you after what you went through out there. I am truly sorry."

Life was too short to hold grudges. "Apology accepted."

"If you want, I'd like to start again." She looked at me hopefully. "I mean, I'd like to be friends."

I could have scoffed and threw it back in her face. I could have rubbed it in. But what kind of person would that make me? I held my hand out to her and said, "Hi, I'm

Prue."

She looked at me confused for a moment, then took my hand. "Hi, I'm Eva."

"Nice to finally meet you," I said with a smile.

Then, to my slack jawed surprise, she wrapped her arms around me in a tight hug. "I wish you and Shaw the best."

"Thank you."

Once she'd disappeared into the crowd, someone cleared their throat behind me. Turning, I found Captain standing with his hands shoved in his pockets looking dour.

"How are you doing?" he asked.

"Fine," I replied.

"You seem brighter today," he nodded towards Shaw, who was talking to a group of men from the wall, Red included.

"He saved my life a thousand times over. I don't know if he understands, but I owe everything to him."

"I think he knows it," he smiled. "You did the same for him, you know."

I thought about all the crap we'd been through since the day we'd met and nodded. I could see Captain looking at me with a puzzled expression, like he was trying to work me out, so I said, "It may seem that I've gotten over it pretty quick, the attack and last night... but one thing I learnt from being out there is how to cope."

"I'd believe that," he smiled.

"How are you?"

"It's hard," he sighed. "They were really good blokes. They'll be sorely missed. And Greg, well... who bloody knows, right?"

To his surprise, I placed a hand on his arm. "It'll never get any easier and it's hard to say goodbye. But, they'll always be remembered."

"What did we ever do without you, Prue?" he sighed, shaking his head.

My eyebrows rose. I'd never expect this from Captain. I guess in a way, he'd become like a father figure, Doc was the fun uncle and Hannah was my older, well adjusted sister. I couldn't pinpoint when, but a whole cast of characters had become my extended family. Hands slid onto my waist and Shaw was beside me.

"I don't know what we did, either," he said with a smile.

Captain grunted, looking across the lawn and I could have sworn he was trying not to cry. "Well, I better leave you kids to it."

"Sure," I said as he wandered away, shaking hands with a few guys as he went.

"He really respects you after the other night," Shaw murmured in my ear. "If you hadn't of been here, it would have been a lot worse."

"I did what had to be done."

He pulled me into his side, planting a kiss on my temple. It still felt strange having his arms around me, but I didn't want him anywhere else. And everyone around us didn't bat an eyelid. It seemed everyone knew we'd end up together, even if we didn't.

Despite the underlying sadness, I smiled as I watched Nan talking to some of the women across the lawn. I was so grateful for everything she'd done for me. She was as much to thank for the person I was evolving into as Shaw, Captain, Doc and Hannah were. Things were finally working out.

My breath caught as Nan clutched at her chest again, her face contorting in pain. Her knees buckled and she fell into the ground, the women around her crying out.

"*Nan*," I exclaimed, Shaw's arm falling away as I rushed forward.

Doc was there a second later, rolling her onto her side. "Breathe, Gwen. In... out..."

"What's wrong?" I asked, falling to my knees beside them trying my best not to panic.

"Shh," Doc calmed me. "She's just had a mild heart attack by the looks of it."

"But..." I began, but I remembered this morning. We should have made her see Doc then. *We should have made her.*

"We need to get her home to bed."

"Prue? Sweetheart?" Nan said, her voice groggy as she started to come around.

"I'm here, Nan," I grabbed her hand. "I'm not going anywhere. I'm going to take care of you."

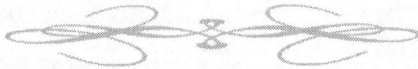

⁂

It was safe to say that the memorial was an even dourer event after that, but I wouldn't know. I hadn't left the house since Doc and Captain brought Nan home. I leant against the wall in the hallway next to an old photo of who

I know knew was a young Nan, Shaw and Captain at my side. It was the photo I'd looked at when I was first able to get around on my own after my leg was stitched up. It had a 1960s looking car with a young Nan sitting on the bonnet. She looked about twenty years old, bright and smiling, her hand raised in a wave.

Doc closed her bedroom door behind him softly and looked up to see us all standing in the hallway. "She needs some rest," he said, gesturing for us to follow him outside.

Once we were all assembled out on the front footpath, he laid it out. "Angina," he said.

"Her heart?" Shaw exclaimed. "How…"

"Angina is a symptom of Coronary Artery Disease," Doc continued. "It's manageable with medication, but it's something we don't have. There's no telling when she might have another attack."

"Then what can we do?" Captain asked.

"She needs to slow down. She needs someone to help her. There's nothing else we can do, especially at her age."

"No," I said, interrupting him. "There must be something else."

"She's pushing eighty, Prue. These things can happen to someone at her age."

"But the medicine…"

"There's nothing to be done about it," Doc said kindly. "I'm sorry, but we just have to manage it best we can."

"But without medicine she'll be in pain," I exclaimed, beginning to get worked up.

"Yes, but…"

"Then we find a hospital."

"Prue, no," Shaw pleaded with me.

I turned to him, a wild look in my eyes. "I'd do anything for her, you know that."

"What if more of those mutants are hanging around? It's a borderline suicide mission."

"What are you talking about?" Doc asked, looking between Captain and us.

"The sick," I said before anyone could say it. "The ones who got better mutated into flesh eating, mindless bags of bones."

"That's not possible." Doc was dumbfounded.

"It's true," Shaw said. "I've seen it with my own eyes."

"Well, I don't care," I declared stubbornly. "If it's the difference to her being in pain or not, then I'm already gone."

I began to stalk away across the street, but Shaw ran after me, grabbing my arm. "Stop."

"No." I jerked away. "I can do this."

"Fuck," he sighed, running a hand over his face. "I know you can do it, but..."

"I'm not arguing with you about this. We've argued enough. I'm not afraid of them. Not anymore."

"Prue you can't," Shaw said, grabbing my arm again, a pained look in his eyes. "I just found you."

"Nan took care of me when she didn't know who I was. She showed me kindness when I could have easily been something else. I owe it to her."

His expression dropped even further. "Well, if you're hell bent on it, then I'm going too."

"Shaw..."

"No, Prue. You said you didn't want to argue anymore. As far as I'm concerned, you and I are a package deal. Where you go, I'm going too."

I hesitated.

"At least come back and talk it through with Doc and Captain. You don't even know what medicine to look for."

"Fine," I sighed, walking back towards the house where Doc and Captain still stood. "But I'm going as soon as I know what I'm looking for."

"We can't go running through the bush at night," Shaw exclaimed, stalking after me. "Do you know how dangerous that can be? You'll fall and break your leg."

"Wait until the early hours," Captain said as we stopped on the footpath. "There's a small hospital in Horsham and it isn't that far. You'll get there with plenty of daylight to get in and out again."

"We can't go there at night, it's even more risky."

"Write a list of the medication," I said, looking at Doc. "We're going at five am. No later." Before they could argue with me further, I went back into the house straight to Nan's bedside. I wouldn't leave her until I had to. I'd carve a hole into the remains of human civilization if it meant easing even a fraction of her pain.

Twenty

"Prue."

I jerked awake, my eyes focusing on Shaw. I'd fallen asleep in the chair next to Nan's bed some time in the night. The windows were tinted with the first signs of dawn, which meant it was time to go. Looking down at Nan, she was still fast asleep.

"C'mon," Saw whispered. "Doc and Captain are here. Then we've gotta go to the cottage."

I rubbed my eyes and tip toed out of Nan's room and into the kitchen, where everyone sat around the table.

"Prue," Doc said as I sat down. "Here's the list." He handed me a piece of paper full of his messy doctor's scrawl. "We need anything with nitroglycerin, aspirin, Sectral, Tenormin, Trandate… any of these are good. Here's the list. There's a lot on it, so grab anything you can put your hands on. In fact, grab everything you can."

"Here's hoping there's something left," Captain said.

I stuffed the list into my pocket and grabbed my sword, which I'd left out on the table last night.

"I can see your mind is made up, Prue, but you don't have to risk yourself like this," Doc said before I could make a break for it.

"I'm going."

"You don't have to go today," Captain said. "We can wait a day and put together a solid plan. Send more men with you."

"No," I shook my head furiously. "Two is already too many. Silence is the best weapon for getting in and out."

"Prue, maybe you should slow down and think about this."

"It's now or not at all." What I didn't want to admit was that I'd lose my nerve if I kept thinking about it. Not wanting to hear anymore arguments against, I stormed towards the front door, Shaw on my heels.

"Prue, Shaw," Doc called out after us. "Be careful, okay?"

"Yes, sir," Shaw nodded and we ran across the town towards the cottage by the gate.

We decided the best course of action was to go straight in and out. Classic snatch and grab. We passed several people on our way and they all looked after us, perplexed. There was no time to stop.

Once we were inside the cottage, Shaw was right beside me, pulling a shotgun from the wall.

"Take a smaller gun," I said. "The lighter the better. If we need to run, you'll thank me. And take a machete. Noise will draw them if they're in the hospital. It'll be dark in there, so they'll be able to move around during the day."

Shaw shivered. "I don't like the idea of close quarters." I guess distance was his thing, being a trained sniper and all.

"I don't like the idea of going into the dark."

"Point."

"I'll do it because I want to. Nan's become my mother. She's cared for me and now it's my turn." I couldn't help the tears that slipped from my eyes.

"Prue," Shaw sighed, wrapping his arms around me. "I'm with you, okay? If I have to imbed a machete in a mutants head, then I'm with you."

"Gross."

He laughed wryly, tossing an empty pack at me and I put a water bottle inside along with some spare ammunition and a small first aid kit. We wouldn't need anything else. Shoving a small handgun through my belt felt strange paired with the weight of the sword on my back. I watched as Shaw strapped a machete to his side. I'd never seen him so armed to the teeth either. Not even out on scout. Then, he'd only had his rifle.

"You better wrap this up," I said taking his beat up hand in mine. "Don't want it getting infected."

Pulling out some bandages from the first aid kit, I began wrapping it up and I felt his other hand brush against my bruised neck.

"Are you sure?" he asked again.

"Yes." I secured the bandage and grabbed my bag. Before I could turn for the door, he grabbed my arm, pulling me back into his chest.

His lips were hard on mine, and when he leant away he said, "One for the road."

Out at the gate, Captain was talking furiously to Bobby, who had a look of confusion on his face.

"But there's no scout until the boys come back," he was saying.

"Let them out," Captain ordered. "They know what they're doing, Bobby. This is for Nan."

He looked at us approaching, then back to Captain and with a shrug, he cracked open the gate enough so we could slip through. "Coast is clear," he said, eyeing the machete and gun at Shaw's waist.

"We should be back just after nightfall," Shaw said. "If we run into trouble, maybe another day."

Captain clapped him on the shoulder. "Just don't take any unnecessary risks." Then he turned to me and to everyone's surprise, he drew me into an awkward hug. "That goes for you too, Prue."

My lips curved into a smile and I nodded and it wasn't until the gate closed behind us that I understood what he meant. I was well and truly a part of this town now.

Horsham was a few hours to the east, and in the half-light it was slow going. We couldn't go as fast as I'd hoped, what with the unanswered question of where those men who'd breached the town came from and the unsteady terrain. The ground was mixed with fallen fence lines, thick bursts of forest and even a few swampy patches, which all made for slow going.

"How do you think we should do this?" Shaw asked as we ran.

"You grew up in Horsham, didn't you?" I asked.

"Yeah." Even though we were breathless, I could still pick up the depression in his voice.

"You never came this way when scouting?"

He shook his head. "Captain knew my family lived out here before. He never once asked me to scout any direction other than north and east."

It was then I realized he'd never seen home since he'd left. I knew all about that. I never went to my families or my own home, but the familiarity in the decay was... there were no words. My heart ached for him.

"It'll be okay," I said. Until this point I'd seen Shaw as the strong one, but even he had lost everything.

We were silent for a while, the only sound the thump of our feet on the dry ground. By the time we came across the first signs of crumbled civilization, it was already well into the morning.

"Shaw?" I called, slowing down to a fast walk. A moment later he was beside me, his heavy breaths loud in the silence.

"I can lead you from here," he said reluctantly. "The hospital is small, but it's a ways into the center of town."

"Okay."

"Do you want to stick to the roads, or..."

"We want the fastest way in," I said. "There's not much we can do about stealth, not outside. Keep to the footpaths and out of the shadows." Out of habit, I checked my sword and the gun that was still firmly through my belt.

"How many times have you been into a town?"

"Three times," I said. "I'm not a font of information, but I know enough about the mutants."

Shaw gave me a look and I scowled at him.

"If we're quiet and fast, then we'll be fine. If push comes to shove, stick 'em with the pointy end."

All he did was grimace and set the pace again.

As we made our way through the edges of the bush and into the city, Shaw kept out in front, so all I could see was his back. If he was put off by being back here, he never said anything. Of course it would be getting to him, it would get to me. The last time he'd have been here it would have been chaos, but before it would have been alive with people and color. Now, it was crumbling and in decay, debris and destruction was growing the closer we got to the city center. Smashed windows, burnt out cars and things that I didn't want to dwell on.

At the end of the street, Shaw squatted at the corner. "The hospital is just around here," he whispered, his eyes widening as they focused on something in the distance.

I flattened my back next to his, my hand on his arm and my eyes followed his. Opposite to where we crouched behind a burnt out car was an old Real Estate office. It's front windows had been partially smashed like all the others had been, but inside was dark. So dark, that I instantly locked onto what Shaw was looking at.

A mutant stood inside the darkness, gently swaying from side to side, it's empty eyes gazing out onto the street.

"Do you think it's seen us?" Shaw whispered in my ear.

"I don't know, but it won't come out here while the sun is out."

I urged him to move along the wall and he scanned the street, looking nervously back at the mutant in the shop front. I swore it was watching us pass, it's empty eyes fixed on our receding forms.

"Clear," Shaw said and he ran across the street, with me at his heels. At the entrance of the hospital the automatic doors were wedged open and cracked. The interior was trashed and empty of life.

"Where do we look?" I asked.

"The wards," Shaw replied. "They should have some kind of storage or pharmacy."

Whatever signs had been on the walls were gone, if there had been any to begin with. The foyer was light and airy, but the halls stretching off of it were massive holes of darkness. My entire body began to tingle even more than that walk through town. Who knew what the hell lurked in here.

We made our way down a corridor to the right, carefully stepping over fallen chairs, paper and broken glass. It was slow work, every opening we came to had to be scanned for movement and searched incase it held a store of medicine or supplies. Every so often we'd hear sounds in the distance - scraping, thuds - that told us we weren't alone. We didn't come across any mutants, but it didn't mean that we should let our guards down.

After about half an hour of searching, I came across a door that looked promising. It sat behind the nurses station and had a great big lock on it and the window that was set into the wood had been smashed in. Gesturing to Shaw, I leant against the wall and slid my hand over the knob.

Cracking the door, I scanned the room, but it was silent and empty. Easing all the way through, I let out a relieved breath. The room had been looted at some stage, but there were still packages and bottles of antibiotics and drugs.

"Shaw," I hissed, gesturing him forward and I instantly began looking for anything that was on Doc's list.

"Is anything here?"

My hand fell onto some packages and I stifled a gasp, recognizing some of the names. "Yes."

"Grab it," Shaw said and dropped his pack and began scooping stuff inside.

We took everything we could put our hands on, stuffing our bags full. There wasn't a great deal left, but enough to warrant a return trip if it was safe enough to do so. This stuff wouldn't just help Nan, it'd help everyone. It was a goldmine.

Both our heads snapped up at the same time as the door began to rattle and my stomach flew into my throat. The glass window that had been in the door was only a small slit and I couldn't see anyone out there, but that meant shit. I motioned at Shaw to hide under the desk, while I ducked behind the cabinet in the corner. There wasn't anywhere else to go. The door creaked open and shuffling footsteps came into the small room, crunching through the granules of glass on the linoleum floor. I bit my lip and my eyes locked with Shaw's. He nodded, a hand grasping the handle of his machete.

Legs stopped right by his hiding place and there was a low whistle and click. He looked back at me again and I shook my head. He couldn't kill it from that angle. It would scream and writhe and bring the whole place down on us. The mutant stood there for so long, I almost thought we'd get away. That was until boney hands shot down and grabbed Shaw's legs, dragging him across the floor and I didn't think twice. I stood out from my hiding place, but the space was too small to draw my sword, so I tore the gun from my belt and fired. The boom was deafening in the silence and the mutant fell with a spray of blood. Shaw's eyes locked on mine, his face ashen, and I held out a hand to help him up.

"We need to run," I said, my voice wavering.

We crashed through the door back into the hall and ran the way we'd come, the whistling sounds of mutants echoing around us. Rounding the corner, two mutants threw themselves across the hall between us. Instinctively, I dropped the gun and drew my sword. Steel bit into flesh as it tried to latch onto me and it fell to the ground, dead. Another came from behind and I beheaded it without breaking stride, but when I turned around for Shaw, he was gone.

"Shaw?" I screeched into the darkness, but all I could hear was the thud of his footsteps as he ran back the way we came.

"Run," I heard him yell back and I knew going after him then would be reckless.

A high pitch squeal snapped me out of my trance and my eyes fixed on a mutant that was running at me from the end of the hall. Drawing my sword, I ducked and swung as it launched itself on me with a single focus on it's deranged mind. Steel bit into flesh and it crashed into the wall behind me, a gaping wound in it's stomach.

It writhed on the floor for a moment, squealing horribly, then it was still. Looking from side to side, I realized I was alone and it was silent. All I could think of was Shaw. Where was he? He could be dead. He couldn't.

Despite his plea for me to run, I searched hall after hall, room after room, but Shaw was nowhere to be found and neither were the mutants that had separated us. My heart thudded painfully at the thought of loosing him. I hesitated in the foyer, my eyes focused on the street outside. The shadows were getting longer and if I didn't make a run for it, I'd be stuck here in the darkness. I'd be dead and have no chance at finding him.

The mutants knew we were here and even if I found somewhere to hide, they would hunt me relentlessly until they'd fed. I had to leave Shaw and get the medicine back to the town and come back at daybreak. That was probably one of the hardest decisions I'd ever had to make. I didn't know if he was alive or dead, but I knew that I loved him. If I died now, then there would be no chance at saving him if he was trapped.

Easing my way out onto the street, I crammed down the tears that threatened to fall and began the painstaking trek through the city. Flattening my back against the shop front opposite the hospital, I peered around the corner, looking for the mutant who had been in the Real Estate office. I cursed as I made out it's boney form in the middle of the street.

My heart ached with so much anger, I just pushed off the wall and ran at it, sword at the ready. At the last second it turned around and I swung, the blade slicing through it's neck. There was no choice now. I had to run.

The city limits grew closer with each step and so did the

sounds of pursuit. I knew they were hunting me and it was the greatest game they'd ever played, but I was smarter. I was faster.

I ran and ran, scrambling over fences, crashing through the bush, stumbling through swamps and after a while, the sounds of the pursuing mutants faded out into the distance. I didn't slow down once I was certain I wasn't being followed anymore. I willed the sun to rise so I could go back and find Shaw. It was my fault he was lost. Mine. If I wasn't so pig headed about helping Nan we could have planned this better. I could have convinced him to let me go alone. I let my emotions make the decision for me. Emotions were what got people killed.

What if I'd gotten Shaw killed? Tears began to stream down my face. I had to turn it off.

As the glow of the town came into view through the trees, it gave me a new burst of speed. As I crashed through the trees, I called out to the silhouette on top the wall. Sliding through the crack in the gate, I ignored the stir I'd created and kept going.

"Prue?" a voice called out, but I didn't hear it and I continued my headlong run all the way to Nan's. There were footsteps behind me, but I didn't care who it was. I had to get the medicine to Nan, then I had to go back.

Crashing through the front door, Doc came out into the hall a surprised look on his face.

"I've got it," I gasped, dumping the bag at his feet.

"Prue?" It was Captain that had called out to me at the gate and now he came through the door behind me, panic in his voice. "Where's Shaw?"

I collapsed on my knees and let out a choked sob. "I don't

know."

Captain was beside me, pulling me into his arms.

"What if he's dead? It's all my fault."

"Shh," Captain murmured, rocking me in his arms. "Shaw's smart. He knows how to handle himself."

"I have to go back. I have to…" I struggled against his arms.

"No. Wait a few hours. Get some rest. There's not much you can do in the dark."

"Come and see Nan," Doc said, a hand on my shoulder. "Have a few hours sleep, then I'll wake you just before dawn."

I stumbled to my feet, wiping away tears with the back of my hand. Doc helped me take my sword off my back and exchanged a look with Captain when he saw the blood that still coated it. I couldn't care what they thought of me then. All I wanted was to see Nan and find Shaw.

Creeping into her room, I was surprised to see her awake. She looked tired and for the first time it really hit me how old she really was. Until now, Nan had seemed indestructible. She was superwoman.

I sat on the edge of the bed and took her hand.

"Are you okay, dear?" she asked, looking me over. I didn't know what I looked like, but it mustn't have been good.

I shook my head.

"You did another selfless thing," she said. "Stupid, but selfless."

"I love you, Nan. Of course I would."

"Prue, you're like my daughter, you know? If I had of known you'd go running around an abandoned hospital, I would have told you to go to your room."

I let out a small laugh, wiping my eyes with the back of a dirty hand. "Nan, Shaw is still out there. I have to go find him."

"I know, dear," she croaked. "He loves you."

"I love him."

She smiled at me then, a tear slipping from her eye. "Then go save him."

Twenty One

The bush was heavy with early morning fog, dew sticking to every available surface. The moisture in the ground had been sucked into the air overnight, throwing a white blanket over the countryside. As I made my way back towards Horsham, I could hardly see more than a hundred meters in any direction. Sunlight was diffused through the mist and it made me worry.

Last night I'd been followed by mutants out into the bush. They could still be out here and without any sunlight nothing would stop them from prowling the bush, waiting.

Passing into the thick forest near the edge of the city I slowed despite my fear for Shaw. In the distance, a branch snapped and my heart stilled. Shadows still loomed in the half-light of dawn and the air felt cooler than it should. I couldn't see any movement between the trees, the milky mist inching its fingers wherever it could. I crouched low anyway, all of a sudden feeling uneasy. Were they still out here looking for me?

This time there was a whistle to my right. I turned toward the sound, thankful for the cover of the ferns around me, but there was nothing there. I knew better to assume it was a bird. Not even a lyre bird who was known to be able to mimic any sound it heard. There were none of those around here.

Wiling myself to freeze, my eyes scanned the forest and I listened, waiting for anything that would give them away. Any clue as to which direction they would come at me. Movement flickered to my right as a mutant darted through the trees. Startled, I began to run through the bush leaping over fallen logs and scrambling over rises, slipping on rotten leaves and mud from the nights dew. This time, I heard sounds of pursuit from behind.

I stopped my headlong rush as a dark form appeared through the trees directly in front of me. Wide eyed and heart thundering I took in the shape of a man, or what had been a man, and drew my sword. No time to stop.

I ran right towards it, aiming my sword directly for it's chest. As the blade sunk into flesh, I pushed the mutant back a few steps before dodging to the side, the movement twisting it around. I kept running forward, using the momentum to wrench the sword free. I heard it drop to the ground, squealing in pain, but I didn't stop to see if it was still alive or not. There was another behind me and I wasn't going to wait for it to catch up.

By the time I reached the edges of the city, I'd lost my pursuer and the mist had lifted enough not to be such a bother and I could move faster. Sunlight lit the streets and its warmth on my shoulders felt like a reprieve. If the mutants were desperate enough they would come out, but chances are they'd stick to darkness for now.

I backtracked the way we'd come yesterday, looking for signs of Shaw just in case, but nothing had changed. When I reached the place where I'd killed the mutant from the Real Estate, I stumbled. There wasn't much left and what was, was the most horrific thing I'd ever seen because it'd once been a human being. Turning sharply, I heaved into the gutter my insides churning. Wiping my face with the back of my hand, I pressed forward, disregarding the remains in the middle of the road.

Lingering at the corner, I scanned the street out front of the hospital and it was clear. I had to search it again to find traces of the way Shaw had gone. He had to be in the hospital. If he wasn't, then I didn't know where the hell he could be.

Inside, I found the place where we'd been separated with no problems. As with the mutant outside, it's friends were in similar shape and I tried not to look. Instead I went the way Shaw had run, looking for a trail I could pick up. The corridor turned sharply to the left a few meters from the intersection and I was greeted with a long open waiting room and another corridor to the right this time. Along one wall was a bank of elevators with signs saying where each floor went and at the rear was a cafeteria of sorts.

Tiptoeing through the lines of seating and over the trash, I made my way forward scanning the floor, always listening to the noises around me. Silence didn't bode well, but neither did sound.

My eyes focused on a dark smear along the corner of the wall where the corridor met the waiting room and my body began to tingle. I knew what I'd find, but I had to confirm. Running a finger through the blood, it was mostly dry but it wasn't congealed like mutant blood. That meant it had to be Shaw's and I felt sick. Pulling out a torch from my pack, I shone it down the hallway into the murky light and it settled on a lump of clothing in the middle of the floor. My insides lurched, but realizing the clothing was red and blue I breathed a small sigh of relief. He'd been wearing his trademark kaki shirt and grey jeans.

I followed the corridor, stopping when I came across another smear of blood on the wall. This time I realized it was a hand print marking the way. Shaw was bleeding and still he left a trail for me. What did that mean?

At the end of the hall was a door leading to the stairwell and I didn't have to shine the torch to see that this was the way he'd gone. A perfect hand print was in the center of the white paint, beckoning. I had no other option but to crack the door and peer into the darkness.

The stairwell was pitch black, so I had no choice but to shine the torch to find the trail again. Shifting the beam upwards, the walls and landing were clear, but angling downwards revealed a smear along the whiteness in the shape of a human hand.

The further I went, the more I thought that Shaw had left the trail for me like he knew he wasn't getting out. It felt like that fairy tale Hansel and Gretel, except I would be finding something more horrible than a child eating witch. Descending down that dark stairwell was the most terrifying thing I'd ever had to do, knowing what could be lying in wait.

At the bottom of the first flight of stairs was another smear of blood along the wall. Shining the torch down the next flight, revealed another, so I descended yet again, footfalls light on the concrete. At the bottom was a door, signaling that this was as far as I was going. The only way now was forward into the basement.

Listening at the door, I couldn't hear any sound coming from the adjoining corridor. Tentatively, I edged it open and shone the torch through the opening, lighting the way. It was empty and I let out a sigh of relief.

Along the hall were several doors, this time the walls were painted grey bricks, which made the light from the torch feel darker than it actually was. Alternating from angling the light upwards and down towards my feet, I made my way along the length of the corridor searching for the blood trail. The first door I came across had a reddish brown handprint right in the middle and my entire body began to tingle. I felt like I was in a horror movie, searching for the serial killer, but the reality was much worse.

The door was labeled with the word *Morgue* and I hoped to god that that wasn't an omen. Edging my way through the opening, I was relieved at least a little when the room was lit with murkily light from outside. A row of small windows lined the side wall hardly large enough to fit my head through let alone crawl out. Stainless steel benches lined the center and cupboards and old halogen lighting rigs filled the space. Some were fallen and smashed on the floor, others were perched precariously against the wall and benches.

Along the left wall was a sliding door that lead to an industrial sized refrigeration unit and beside it was about half a dozen individual doors for bodies that were kept in storage.

The metal was smeared with semi-dry blood and there were deep dents where mutants had tried to get inside without luck. Shaw must have locked himself behind one of those doors. Shoving the torch in my back pocket, I ran across the room, heart in my throat at the realization that there wouldn't be any air inside. It was a morgue and the doors would have seals on them to prevent decomposition. My hands slapped against the handle, wrenching open the steel door and I gasped in horror. Shaw was lying inside, his clothes stained with blood and he looked awfully still. I pulled the drawer out, straining against the stiff runners that screeched a little too loud in the silence.

"Shaw?" His eyes were closed and his skin felt clammy to the touch. I pressed my index and middle finger to his neck, feeling for a pulse. Please, please, please. I sighed in relief when I found a small flutter, regular but faint.

There was a lot of blood on him and I hoped to hell it wasn't his. I checked all of his limbs, chest stomach, but only came back with scrapes and a few cuts. A gash on his temple was probably the source. Head wounds were gushers no matter how shallow. I placed a shaking hand on his forehead and willed him to wake up.

"Shaw? Please wake up, Shaw..." I pressed my lips to his, not sure what to do. There was no way I was strong enough to carry him out of here. Even if I made some kind of stretcher, the noise it'd make scraping along the floor would be horrendous.

After a moment of panic, his eyes fluttered and I couldn't stop the tears of relief from flooding down my face. There were those green eyes I'd become so familiar with staring up at me.

"I knew you'd come," he rasped.

"I'm sorry," I whispered. "I left you... I..."

"It's okay." His clammy hand was fumbling for mine. "You came back."

"Let's get out of here," I said, helping him up off the metal slab. "Are you hurt?"

"Just a couple of bruises."

"Your head..."

"It's just a flesh wound," he grimaced, steadying himself against the wall. "The bleeding has stopped."

"We can't rest," I said, fisting my hands in his shirt. "We have to get out now or not at all. Can you walk?"

"I'm just light headed." He wiped his brow and I handed him my water bottle. Taking a long draught, he nodded that he was ready. He had to be.

He'd dropped his pack somewhere along the way, but still had the machete strapped to his belt. Right now I didn't care about the medicine we'd lost, I was grateful I'd found him. Now we just had to make it home alive.

I led the way out of the basement back into the semi-darkness of the hospital's upper floors, Shaw's hand in mine, listening for any traces of mutants. So far, we'd been lucky and by the time we reached the foyer our luck was about to run out.

Flattening my back against the wall of the adjoining hall, I peered around the corner and instantly saw three mutants lingering at the automatic door, scratching at the broken glass. They seemed too stupid to realize they could just step over the debris and come right inside, but I knew that once they saw us, they'd have no trouble falling over each other to get in.

The fact that they were there at all was a huge pain in the ass. They knew we were here and they were desperate enough to brave the sun to sate their hunger. Where there were three, there'd be ten more waiting out in the street and twenty more after that. We weren't just up shit creek. We were at the source.

"Three at the door," I murmured into Shaw's ear. "They knew I came back."

He gave me a confused look.

"They were out in the forest," I whispered. "Somehow they followed me and were waiting when I came back."

"Shit," Shaw hissed, leaning back against the wall. "How many?"

"I don't know. I killed one, but it sounded like there was at least another, maybe more."

"We just have to go while there's still light. No stopping." He grabbed my hand and squeezed.

"I love you," I said, my eyes fixed on his. Seemed like a good time to say it.

He cupped my face and covered my mouth with his, kissing me like it was going to be the last time. Maybe it was, but we weren't going to go out without one hell of a fight.

"Whatever happens next, I love you," he said, voice husky as I pressed my gun into his hands.

"Machete," I said, lips against his. "Use the gun as a last resort."

"I'm right behind you."

Twenty Two

As soon as we stepped out into the foyer the mutants launched themselves at us with a mindless hunger I didn't know humans were capable of. All frothing mouths and wide unseeing eyes. But, were they really human anymore? Who knew. All I was certain of was that they wanted to eat us and I wanted to live. I'd never wanted to live so much in my entire life. For Nan, for Hannah, for the town, for *Shaw*. I'd gotten him into this mess and it was my responsibility to get him out.

I motioned for Shaw to stand back as I pulled my sword free, swinging as the first mutant lunged. I cut into it's neck with an accuracy that surprised even me and it dropped with a high-pitched scream, but I didn't have time to deal a killing blow to silence it. The second mutant was right behind it and this time I dropped to a knee arcing the blade back around, tearing through bone and emancipated flesh like butter. I was on my feet in an instant, sinking the sword deep into its back.

A screech behind me snapped me to my senses as I realized the third had gotten around me as I cut down its friends. My thoughts instantly went to Shaw, but I should have been more worried about myself. Pivoting on my heel with a horrified gasp, I knew I wasn't going to angle my sword in time. That split second before something bad happens, everything goes in slow motion. I mean, you can see it coming for ages and do nothing about it, but as fast as the mutant's hands and teeth came at me it stopped mid-stride, it's squeal of rage cut off.

As it fell to the ground, I looked up into Shaw's eyes, his machete well and truly embedded in the skull of the mutant.

"I've got you," he said, shoulders heaving. He was oddly exhausted from such a short burst of energy and I knew he was feeling the effects of his night in the morgue more than he was letting on.

"Thanks," I said through a sharp sigh of relief.

He reached down and pulled the machete free and it came back with a sucking sound that made me sick to the stomach. "Let's keep going."

Outside the street was empty, but that didn't mean anything. Those three had turned up out of nowhere and it was safe to say that there would be more lying in wait. The quickest way out into the bush was the way we'd come, but I was beginning to think we should take another route.

"Is there another way we can go?" I whispered.

"Yeah," Shaw said. "But it'll take longer to get out. It's more residential. If we go the other way we'll be stuck on the other side of town and have to go all the way around."

"It'll have to do."

He didn't ask about my change in plans and I knew him well enough to know that he got it. Our escape route had been compromised and I'm sure that was a tactic used in the army. Alternatives, fail-safes, that kind of thing.

As we made our way from the hospital, we kept as close to the sides of buildings as we could, not chancing anything. Scanning shop fronts and openings took more time, but I wasn't going to leave anything to chance.

Every time we heard the slightest of noises, we'd take cover. Behind a car, in someone's front yard. We'd stop and listen, not wanting to risk an open fight. The mutant's desperation for food was driving them to do whatever it took and that was a thought too much to handle.

"What's the time?" I asked, looking at the sky.

"Four," Shaw said, a note of worry in his voice. "There's probably an hour of light before it'll start getting dark."

And I knew it meant it would get dark very quickly after that. The days were getting shorter in the lead up to winter. It'd be pitch black by six o'clock and with Shaw as beat as he was we wouldn't be back to the town in time. They'd follow us and I'd doubt that we'd be able to out run them this time.

"No matter," I said. "It is what it is." Shaw sighed behind me and I felt for his hand. "It's my fault we were out here in the first place. It was my fault..."

He jerked me back into his chest, silencing me. "It is what it is. I don't blame you."

"I let my emotions in and it led us right into this mess."

"I don't blame you."

"We don't have time for this," I hissed.

"It's not a bad thing to have emotions," he said.

No, maybe not, but that was yet another thing I had to work on. Turning around, I kissed him on the lips. "We'll argue about this later."

"And I look forward to making up with you," he grinned as if we weren't in a shitload of trouble.

We continued through the streets of forgotten houses, the eerie lack of movement tingling up and down my spine. I'd never get over how empty the world was now. Seeing it in movies and reading about it in books didn't have anything on seeing it in real life. I almost expected to see ghosts in the streets going about their daily business. Driving to work, delivering the mail, but there was no one.

"Where are they?" Shaw asked, voicing the creeping feeling that had been growing in the pit of my stomach. Where were the mutants?

"I don't know."

"The bush?"

"Maybe."

"They're waiting for the dark..." Shaw began, a look of horror on his face. They were waiting for the dark when they could hunt us in openly and in numbers. I didn't know if that was a sign of lingering intelligence or some kind of animal instinct, but I didn't want to find out.

"Can you run?" I asked, suddenly panicked.

"I'm a little beat," he said, finally owning up to the fact he wasn't feeling right. "But, there's no other choice."

"You go first," I said. "I'll follow. We need to make up as much ground as we can before it gets dark."

Scanning the street once more, he moved off at a jog. The only sound that pierced the silence was our footfalls on the asphalt as the town began to thin out around us. Every so often Shaw would slow to a fast walk, his breath ragged.

The town passed into the bush as the sun began to set, the clouds overhead tinted an otherworldly orange. Now that we were out in the open, we were being followed openly. Without cover, they could track us easily and keep a distance until they had us in a position where they could attack. Our only option was the same as it had been since we left the hospital. Keep moving.

"I need to rest a moment," Shaw gasped, coming to a halt. He lent over, hands on his knees, breathing heavily.

"We can't stop," I said, my eyes scanning the darkening bush.

"Just a minute."

Both our heads snapped up as a sharp click and whistle pierced the air and everything that I'd assumed up until now was suddenly confirmed.

"How the hell did it track us out here?" Shaw exclaimed.

I raised a hand to his temple and he hissed when my fingers brushed the wound that was clogged with dry blood. "This."

"Fuck."

"It'll be okay, Shaw," I said. "If it comes for us, then I'll take care of it."

He took my hand and pulled me close, lips against my forehead. "Thank you."

"Thank me when we get home," I said.

"If we weren't still in the shit I'd say something about that."

"About what?"

"Home."

I grabbed his hand and pulled him forward, leading the way. There wasn't any time to contemplate that. "Tell me if you hear or see anything," I said. "No matter how small."

"Fuck, I love how you take charge," he said behind me and I wondered if that knock on his head had gotten to him. Trying to have a relationship with Shaw would be anything but dull. I'd imagine we'd argue till we were blue in the face then have a hell of a time making up afterwards.

We didn't get very far before there was another whistle on the air, this time from behind to the left and a moment later, an answering one from the right.

"We have to fight it," I said, stopping in the middle of a small clearing. Either we take it out or it would run us down.

"What?"

"There's no other way. If we keep moving, then it'll take us." He went to hand the gun back to me, but I curled my fingers around his.

"What about you?" he asked, looking at me in concern.

"I'm better with my sword. You know I can't shoot very well." He was the one with the military training and I hoped it would come in handy right about now.

He nodded reluctantly. "They're close," he whispered. "If we're gunna stand and fight, it better be back to back. They'll probably try and surround us."

My skin suddenly felt clammy and I nodded.

"I love you."

"I love you."

Movement flashed through the trees, circling in our location. I felt Shaw's back tense against mine as the whistle and click of the mutants called to each other. How many there were, there was no way of telling. We had to stand and fight until there were no more.

A screech ripped apart the air as the first mutant lunged and I swung my sword upwards, stepping forward and away from Shaw's back. Steel bit into flesh, cutting of its awful wail. The next wasn't far behind, the boom of the gun going off almost bursting my eardrums.

I stepped back into Shaw, regrouping, waiting for the next wave that was all but imminent. We could hear them out in the darkness, hiding, watching, waiting for the moment when they could strike.

"Are you okay?" Shaw broke the silence first.

"I'm okay."

"How many do you think are out there?" He sounded strong, sure, but even I was peeing my pants a little.

Listening to the sounds from the surrounding bush it felt like there was about a dozen, but I knew better than anyone how sound could distort out here. They were constantly moving, trying to confuse us. I hoped that the fact that we understood their tactics would see us coming out on top in the end.

"Maybe six or so. They're trying to confuse us." As soon as the last word left my lips, a mutant broke through the undergrowth on my right and before I could move, Shaw shot it right between the eyes.

"Not such a shit shot anymore," he said wryly as it fell to the ground, twitching.

The reference to our first meeting didn't go unnoticed as I elbowed him in the back. A branch snapped directly in front of me and another mutant threw itself towards us and I flew into motion without blinking. Arcing the sword with all the strength I could muster, the blade sunk into its neck, imbedding into bone. The force dragged me down to one knee as the mutant hit the earth, pain jarring up my leg into my hip. With a grunt, I pulled the sword free and brought it down again, severing its head from its body. On my feet a split second later, Shaw fired behind me, felling another as I pivoted on my heel.

My eyes widened as I came face to face with what once was a woman, lank, stringy blonde hair stuck to a gaunt face with unseeing eyes. Teeth and clawed hands came at me and I stumbled back a step before bringing the sword up to defend myself. As I felt steel hit flesh, its face stopped inches from mine before letting out a wail that reverberated right into my soul.

Letting out a gasp that was part horror, part relief, I pushed the mutant off my sword, it's limp body hitting the ground with a thud. My head snapped up as the gun went off again, a squeal cut off sharply moments from reaching its goal.

Shaw stumbled a step, his hand over his arm, the gun shaking in the other.

"Shaw?"

"It's nothing," he said. "Just a bruise."

The forest was finally silent around us, the air thick with blood and gunpowder. I curled my fingers around Shaw's, the same hand that I'd wrapped up over a day ago now.

The bandage was lose and caked with dirt and blood and he wasn't much better. It might have been the moonlight, but I knew he was fading.

"We need to move," I said. "More will come."

"I know." He wiped his brow with the back of his free hand, smearing blood across his face.

I took the gun from his hand, clicked on the safety and shoved it through his belt. His eyes were glassy and he wore a dazed expression that gave away just how beat he was.

"Tell me if you need to stop." I wound my fingers through his and he nodded.

We set off again through the bush, leaving behind the carnage in the darkness. The forest was behind us, and we were soon crossing the swamp, our boots sticking in mud, making it slow going. In the distance a high pitched screech pierced the night and I knew that more mutants had found the remains of our stand.

Shaw's hand tightened around mine and we just had to keep pushing. We were both at the end of our strength and the only thing that kept us going was the thought of what waited for us at home. It had been such a strange notion, but it's what it was. Home.

We climbed over fences, crossed paddocks, stumbled and fell more times that we could count, but one thing drove us both. The fact that we wanted to live. All that time ago, I was prepared to lay down where I stood and just die. I'd reached the end of my will to care, to go on, to survive and now I had everything to live for. It was love that drove us now, not strength or desire or even an animal instinct. *Love*. It was such a strange thing.

The moment I was beginning to think that we'd be wandering the bush in the wrong direction was the moment I saw it. A warm orange glow shone through the trees and relief hit me like a tsunami. We broke through the tree line and I whistled, the sound piercing the air like a knife. When the answering call came, I pulled Shaw in front, my eyes on the darkness behind, but nothing was there. If anything had followed, they knew better than to attack here.

The gate scraped open and Shaw stumbled forward, his shoulder slamming against the corrugated iron. The moment we were inside, he fell to his knees, utterly exhausted. I was beside him in an instant, flinging my pack and sword to the side. I was sure there were people around us, Captain, Bobby... but as I circled my arms around Shaw, he was the only one I had eyes for.

"We're home," I said, burying my face into his neck. "We're home."

What Remains

After Shaw and I ran into town so dramatically, the Mayor was forced to disclose the truth about the mutants and what the virus had wrought on the survivors. One day we'd have to face them, but thankfully that day wasn't today. We now had the means and the knowledge to deal with them when the time came.

Some of the men were eager to help rigging some defenses for the wall and everyone chipped in with ideas. There was a lot of talk about motion sensors and what not and I wasn't sure how they were going to do it, but the idea sounded brilliant in theory. I could see a lot of false alarms from stray kangaroos and the wind, but it was a start.

When the men came back from scouting the intruder's camp it wasn't all good news. They found no sign of life and no sign to say Greg's sister had been there at all. But, if the man I'd held at the edge of my sword that night was telling the truth… then she'd been dead for almost two years. There was no real way of telling if she'd ever been there in the first place.

They'd dismantled the camp and brought back anything that was useful. Guns and ammunition, food that had obviously come from the town and some of their camping gear.

And Greg? Well, once the men came back with their report, the town came together in a vote to decide his fate. It was close, but he was given permission to stay, with severe rations and duties. Four men had died because of his intel and that wasn't easily forgotten. He'd be paying for it with regret and suffering every single day for the rest of his life. Sending him out to a life like I'd led for so many years... not even I could do it to him, even though I'd wanted to. It was a death sentence and none of us wanted to be an executioner.

With the medication Shaw and I found in the hospital and a reduced workload, Nan was able to manage her condition with little pain. She'd scolded us severely for putting ourselves in danger for her, but I pretended not to hear. The day would come when she would no longer be here, but there would be one of those for all of us eventually. For now, she was with us and that was all that mattered.

After everything that had happened, it was safe to say that I was now a fully fledged member of the town. I was so ingrained in the woodwork, people sought me out to thank me for all the things I had done for them. Not only with the intruders, but bringing back the medicine. It was things like this that helped, but one day we'd have to manage without. The town had to adapt and that's what would ultimately ensure our survival.

Shaw and I? Well, it was just as I'd imagined. We'd argue every other day and then... well you can imagine. We were in love and at the beginning of the world, not at the end anymore. I cursed everything we'd had to go through to find each other, but the day he'd tried to shoot me was one of the best days of my life. Sounds messed up, but that was the day Shaw saved my life. I owed him everything and I'd do whatever it took to show him every single day.

We were okay for now and that's all we were really certain of. We had each other and that was a start. The rest would come in time.

What remained now was hope.

I'd never known true darkness until the lights went out.

But, I'd never known true love until they came back on.

About the Author

Nicole R. Taylor is a paranormal, urban fantasy and contemporary fiction author from Ballarat, in Victoria, Australia.

Previously, she has written for various small street press music and entertainment publications as a gig and album reviewer before publishing her first Urban Fantasy novel in early 2013.

When she isn't writing, Nicole likes to spend time curled up with a good book and her 3 year old rescue cat, Burger. She gets itchy feet more often than not and has lived in three countries and travelled to three times as many.

Learn more about her writing at:
www.nicolertaylorwrites.com

She may be contacted by email at:
nicole.this.is@gmail.com

OTHER BOOKS BY NICOLE R. TAYLOR

The Devil's Tattoo (Devil's Tattoo #1)

What Remains

The Witch Hunter Saga

The Witch Hunter (#1)

The Return (#2)

The Shadow's Son (#3)

TITLES COMING SOON...

The Fire Walker (Devil's Tattoo #2) (December 2013)

The Awakening (#4 in the Witch Hunter Saga) (early 2014)

For more info go to www.nicolertaylorwrites.com

Printed in Great Britain
by Amazon.co.uk, Ltd.,
Marston Gate.